Carnage

Jan-Andrew Henderson

Black Hart

Edinburgh. Brisbane.

First published 2019 by Black Hart

Black Hart Entertainment.
Blackhartentertainment.com

Cover by Panagiotis Lampridis (BookDesignStars)
Book Layout © 2017 BookDesignTemplates.com

Carnage.
ISBN 978-1-64570-605-2 (Print)
ISBN 978-1-64570-606-9 (eBook)

If only one man dies of hunger, that is a tragedy.
If millions die, that's only statistics.

Attributed to Joseph Stalin

For Scarlet the Brave

-1-

It is my opinion that the children of the village rose up in the middle of the night and slaughtered the adult population in their sleep.

Then they ate them.

Major Dron highlighted the final lines of the report with a yellow pen. He still couldn't get to grips with what it said.

"Is your commander a moron?" he asked the soldier guarding the tent. "You have my permission to speak freely."

"Sergeant Heatherly?" The man remained ramrod straight, eyes fixed on the dusty flap opening, as it snapped back and forwards in the wind. "He's a solid bloke. Does things by the book."

"You wouldn't say he had an overactive imagination?"

The eyes flickered briefly towards Major Dron before fastening back on the entrance.

"I asked you a question, soldier."

"As far as I know, he doesn't have *any* imagination. He's in the army."

The Major didn't smile.

"Read this to me." He held out the report to the guard. "I want to see your reaction."

"I can't, Sir." The man sounded suitably startled. "It says **Highly Classified** on the cover. I'm only a private."

"That's not a request. It's an order."

Major Dron had never done things by the book. He was fairly sure that was why he'd ended up in a dump like Birjand.

The soldier took the folder, opened it and began to read aloud, glancing every now and then at his superior.

We arrived in the village at 07.00 hours, after a distress call made by satellite phone from Margaret Mead, a field worker with Christian Aid Abroad. Our unit could find no sign of Ms Mead or, indeed, any adults. We encountered no hostiles - but all livestock had vanished from the corral and the buildings appeared damaged by mortar fire.

The village children, however, were unharmed. They hugged my men and held out their hands, begging for food. We put down our arms to distribute chocolate bars and what spare rations we had. Suspecting there had been a bandit attack, the Lieutenant inspected the buildings to try and ascertain what kind of weapons any potential enemy possessed. He shouted that it was impossible, of course, but the damage looked like it had been done by bite marks.

That's when the children attacked.

They threw themselves at my men, using their teeth to try and inflict maximum injury. We grabbed our weapons and fought them off with the butts of our rifles but were heavily outnumbered. When I saw the Lieutenant torn to pieces by a group of fifteen children or more, I reluctantly ordered my men to open fire.

Once we had contained the situation, we locked the surviving children in one of the larger buildings. Unfortunately, they ate their way through the wall and we had to contain the situation again.

"Contain the situation?" Major Dron ran a hand down his face. "You massacred a bunch of kids! And what does he mean by *ate their way through the wall*?"

"I tried to push one away with my rifle." The soldier swallowed hard. "He bit right through it. I know it sounds crazy but his jaw opened so wide it was like a snake swallowing a football."

"You can see how I'd find this version of events difficult to accept." The Major snatched back the report. "Can't you?"

"You should see what's left of Lieutenant Lovelock." The guard's face turned to granite. "You'll find that even harder to accept."

Major Dron was about to reprimand the man for his curtness when the flap was pushed back and sergeant Heatherly shouldered his way in. The man saluted then stood to attention – a broad shouldered veteran with sand matted hair.

"I want an explanation for what happened here," the Major began, not bothering to return the salute. "A better one than the rubbish I've just been reading. I cannot believe you thought…"

"With all due respect, Sir," Heatherly interrupted. "You need to come and see this."

He turned on his heel and left the tent. His superior hesitated, stunned by the man's insubordination. Then he went after him.

"Are you trying to dig yourself a deeper hole?" he fumed, catching up with the sergeant. "You could be up on charges of war crimes because of this little stunt!"

"There's a cave just behind the village. Probably used for smuggling opium." Heatherly didn't slow down or even look over his shoulder. "We put the remaining children in there and sealed the entrance with rocks but it's only a matter of time before they break out."

"Sealed them in with rocks?" Major Dron grabbed the man's arm. "Are you insane?"

"Get your hand OFF me." The sergeant spun round, his eyes glittering with fear. "I lost three men yesterday, including my Lieutenant. You can discharge me. Court Martial me. Arrest me. I don't care. But you'll damned well come and see what we've got here before you say another word."

He strode off again. The Major followed, shaking with anger but at a loss for what else to do.

Heatherly's men stood in a ring round the entrance to the cave, pointing their weapons at a pile of boulders blocking the way in. All were silent and ashen faced. They still had crusted blood on their faces and uniforms. Water was a scarce commodity around these parts.

"The children are in there," Heatherly said blankly. An ominous crunching sound emanated from behind the makeshift barricade.

"Should we pile more rocks on?" one of the men asked, rifle shaking in his hand. "They're almost through."

"You will not." Major Dron retorted, outraged. "In fact, take away the ones blocking the entrance right now. You want to start an international incident?"

The soldier ignored the outburst.

"Should we pile more rocks on, Sarge?" he repeated.

"No lad." Heatherly shook his head sadly. "The Major wants to see the kiddies. He's in charge now."

The crunching sound rose in volume. Heatherly's soldiers cocked their weapons and raised them to their shoulders. The boulders began to slowly move, pebbles cascading down the uneven surface.

Major Dron held his breath.

Then the children burst through. Their clothes were in tatters, their skin mottled and red with blisters.

But it was the mouths the Major fixed on. The jaws widened like the shovels of mechanical diggers, opening so far they obscured the children's scrawny chests and forced their eyes into malign slits.

Each gaping maw was ringed by ragged teeth, grimy with dirt and stained by mucus and blood.

"Oh dear Lord," Major Dron whispered, unholstering his sidearm

With each massive bite, the children tore chunks from the rock pile and spat them out in pieces. Boulders tumbled over each other until there was a gap big enough for the rest of the tiny prisoners to scramble out.

Soon, a scrawny rabble faced the soldiers, heads bowed and fists clenched.

Then the children looked up, opened their terrible mouths, and charged.

"Open fire!" The Major screamed, pulling free his weapon as the mass of half human urchins loped towards him. "For God's sake, open fire!"

Sergeant Heatherly nodded grimly and the air was filled with the sound of automatic weapons.

When the carnage was over, Major Dron ordered the bodies left on the stone floor and the cave blown up.

The next day, he was transferred to Somalia.

-Part One-

Under normal conditions, in their natural habitats, wild animals do not mutilate themselves, attack their offspring, develop stomach ulcers, suffer from obesity or commit murder... Does this, then, reveal a basic difference between the human species and other animals?

At first glance it seems to do so. But this is deceptive. Other animals do behave in these ways under certain circumstances - namely when they are confined in the unnatural conditions of captivity.

Desmond Morris. *The Human Zoo.*

-2-

A ceremony announcing the winner of the 'Young Scot Bravery Award' was to take place in Edinburgh Zoo next week. The management had offered a year's free entry as first prize and today was the dress rehearsal.

The stand-in judges were keepers who hadn't thought of a decent lie to get out of the job and considered the whole thing a complete waste of their time. But it was a nice bit of press for the zoo, even though only two reporters bothered to turn up and cover the run-through.

Since almost everyone would be dead by noon, this turned out to be a lucky break for the no-shows.

Before the practise presentation, fifteen finalists were given stickers with their names on and shepherded into the zoo's café for breakfast.

The teenagers at table three looked warily at each other. None of them had met before and the early hour and formal setting weren't ideal for getting acquainted. Most had been sent by their schools, forced to attend by overenthusiastic teachers who fancied borrowing a free pass if their pupil won.

"Does anybody know what this *is*?" A black clad boy finally broke the silence, pulling a slab of meat from his sandwich and waving it at his companions. He lifted a swathe of blue streaked hair off his forehead and peered at the slice in horror.

"Nasty shit, eh? It springs back into shape when you bend it."

His sticky tag bore the name JAMES WILBER-FORCE but he had scored it out in blue pen and written MONDO underneath.

"It's giraffe," his neighbour said solemnly. He wore a hooded top and his tag said WILL OAKLEY. "I seen there was one missing since the last time dad dragged me here. Probably died of boredom."

"I know how it feels."

"Nope. This is a squirrel," the girl to the left piped up, removing the mystery meat and hiding it under her paper plate.

"How d'you figure?"

"Cause it's grey and you'd have to be nuts to eat it."

She was short and sturdy, with a stunning face, wide brown eyes and a name tag that said JULIANNE BU-CHANAN.

There was an awkward silence while the trio tried to open a new avenue of conversation.

"So, what did you all do to get nominated for a bravery award?" Will Oakley finally asked.

"Chased away a couple of thugs who were trying to snatch an old lady's bag." Julianne smiled pleasantly. "You?"

"Jumped in the Union Canal to save a toddler after he lost control of his trike."

"Nice one."

"Not really. It's only four feet deep. Ruined me new trainers, though."

"Price of being a hero, Will." Julianne took a slurp of her orange juice. "Call me Joolz."

"Name's Oakley." The boy winked at her. "Wills are something you write when you're going to die."

An Indian teenager peeled himself away from the end of the table and sauntered over. He had on an impeccable red blazer, buttoned to the top, with a neatly pressed shirt and striped tie underneath.

"Hello there, fellow champions." He slapped his sandwich on the table in front of the others. "Anyone want to swap my unpalatable snack for an apple? I am a vegetarian."

Stuck to his forehead was a label saying AKILAN.

"Here ya go." Oakley tossed his fruit to the boy. "How come you only got one name?"

"Maybe they think I am like Rihanna." Akilan nodded towards the teacher's table, where a group of adults stared dolefully at cardboard snack boxes decorated with penguins. "Either that or my bloody surname is too long to fit on the tag."

"What is it?"

"Channarayapatra."

"You're never going to bag the prize, mate," Oakley whistled. "It would take too long to read that out."

"You also have one name." Akilan squinted at Mondo's badge. "Do I sense a kindred spirit?"

"Not if you win." The boy sat back and stretched. "I better get something out of this crappy boast-fest. They confiscated my DS on the bus."

"Mine too," Oakley nodded. "I was playing a game where you hunt endangered species. You get 1,000 points for a panda."

"Your sarcasm is noted." Akilan bit into his apple. "I am not pleased to end up here either. Valiant though I may be, I am allergic to animals."

A teacher with a few slicked strands of hair covering the top of his head got to his feet and coughed loudly.

"Right then, people," he announced. "The zoo is open to the public now and visitors are filing in. So let's finish up and make our way over to the old manse where the prize giving ceremony will be held. It's in a marquee next door!"

"What's a marquee?" Oakley asked. "Baldy seems awful excited about it."

"It's a big tent."

"Oh." The teenager didn't share his teachers' enthusiasm. "It'll be cold then."

"Once the winner and two runners-up have been announced, you'll be getting a tour of the zoo." The man gave a near manic grin. "How exciting is that?"

"Not much point winning a pass if we're going to see the damned place anyway," Mondo complained. "I've got Discovery Channel. You can watch a tiger on that close up. In this joint, it'll be sleeping in some dingy cave behind three feet of streaky glass."

"Chin up. Maybe it will escape today." Akilan draped scrawny arms round the shoulders of his new companions. "Give us all a bit of a chase, hey?"

"I'd be ok." Joolz finished the last of her orange juice with a slurp. "I hold my school's record for the hundred metres."

"That is impressive, yes." Akilan yawned. "But I don't think you are going to be as fast as a tiger."

"I don't need to be as fast as the tiger." Joolz crumpled up the carton and tossed it expertly in the bin.

"I just need to run quicker than you lot."

-3-

Bangles and his friend, Rerun, climbed down their home made ladder into the zebra paddock, leaving a knotted length of rope dangling from the perimeter wall. The zebras were at the outskirts of Edinburgh Zoo, on top of a steep hill, sharing their huge field with a herd of Thomson's gazelles. The creatures occupied this large isolated location so they had enough land to graze - and because people preferred to see the big cats.

The teenagers hit the ground with a thud and rolled, commando style, behind the nearest bush. Both boys were black, wearing Tommy Hilfiger tops and jeans slung so low they almost defied gravity.

Bangles scrambled back on his hands and knees to retrieve loose change that had erupted from various pockets before diving for cover again.

"Shouldn't we pull that down, dawg?" Rerun lay on his back and looked uncertainly at the rope. "We aint going out the way we come in, anyhows."

"S'all good," Bangles said nonchalantly. "Nobody gonna clock it at this distance when it be the same colour as the wall."

He set his tractor cap at a jaunty angle, peak to the rear.

"We do what we come for, climb over the gate at the other end an ghost into the zoo. Mingle with the crackers, you feel?"

"I dunno, cuz. Bet we don look like the dudes that normally come to dis crib. Not exactly gonna blend in."

"Chill. Dere's nobody here yet. S'too early. Besides, zebras and dem horny things be too boring to draw a crowd."

"Dose zeebs kick an bite, bro. I seen it on TV. Or else they juss run away."

"That's why I brung the sugar lumps." Bangles pulled a handful of white cubes from his pocket. "All horses be fiendin for sugar lumps. And zebras just be li'l horses with stripes."

He gave a huge grin.

"Think of it as connecting with our roots."

"We from Chicago, dawg. Didn't expect to be goin on no safari."

"Exactly! It *look* like the real deal." Bangles licked his fingers and wiped his hi-tops, frowning at the green stains. "We gonna film yours truly sittin on one of dose stripy mothers an rappin. Then we upload it to You Tube and get a million hits!"

He pulled a tiny video camera from inside his jacket.

"Boo ya! I be viral in a hot minute, score a record contract and my music career be set to bubble. Feel?"

"Still don't see why you need me, braw."

"Who's gonna work the camera? One of the ante-lopes?" Bangles picked the last few blades of grass from his jacket and squared his shoulders. "You set to man up an hold me down?"

"You know it."

"Then gets your swerve on, fore anyone spots us." Signalling the discussion was over, Bangles pulled his friend out of their hiding place and strode purposefully towards the herd of zebras.

"Hey, check dis." Rerun thumped his friend on the shoulder. "Dose mad critters aint running away at all. Dey comin towards us!"

He looked round.

"So are the big deer, bro. You think dey smell the sugar or juss bein friendly?"

Bangles stopped.

"Something's not right," he murmured.

"What? Dey all trottin right over. Iss what we want, innit?"

"I watch the Nature Channel, son." The sugar lumps fell from Bangles' hand. "They shouldn't oughtta be doin that."

The zebra herd suddenly broke into a gallop, heading straight for them.

"Dey charging!" Fear crept into Rerun's voice. "An acting all screepy."

"Pack it up, right now!" Bangles commanded. "Dat tree. Get into dat tree!"

The teenagers sprinted for a towering acacia, Bangles stuffing the camera into his jacket as he ran. He was taller and faster than Rerun and reached refuge while the zebras were still twenty feet away. Hitting the trunk, he scrambled into the lower branches, turning to reach out for his companion.

The teenager's eyes bulged in horror.

The gazelles had joined in the chase, easily outstripping the zebras. They were right behind Rerun, a sea of bouncing brown backs and bobbing horns.

"C'mon, homie." Bangles seized a branch and reached out. "Jump, Rerun! Use you ups!"

Rerun reached the tree and began to climb. A gazelle leapt into the air and caught his jeans with one horn. The boy gave a yelp of terror as he was jerked away from the acacia, pleading hand inches from his friend's outstretched fingers.

Then he was gone, trampled under dozens of razor sharp hooves.

"Aw… naw, naw, naw!" Bangles pressed his face against the bark and closed his eyes.

When he finally opened them, his friend's broken body lay motionless in the churned up mud. He felt bile rise in his throat.

The zebras and gazelles were standing in a ring around the tree, staring at him.

Bangles scrambled higher into the branches and pointed his finger.

"Bam, bam," he rasped, clicking his thumb at the motionless beasts. "You aint gonna get away with killin my bestie, feel me?"

He gave a shuddering sob.

"You motherfuckers gonna pay."

-4-

Inside the zoo's control centre, Connor Lane demolished a Mars bar while he switched on the banks of CCTV screens that kept watch over each enclosure. Behind him, the few keepers who weren't acting as judges prepared for the day ahead. Plastic cups, chocolate wrappers and torn sugar sachets covered the low circular table.

"You animals better clean up when you're finished," Connor admonished. "I'm not your personal slave."

There was a chorus of objections from the lounging staff and an empty plastic cup hit him on the back of the head. The supervisor didn't give them the satisfaction of turning round to see who had done it. Plenty of other ways to get his own back.

"Hey, Donna!" He called over his shoulder. "The CCTV monitoring enclosure four is on the fritz."

"Aw, I just sat down, Con." A portly redhead bit into a biscuit and wiped crumbs from her blue overalls. "Give the console a thump."

"First thing I tried. C'mon, it's just next door."

"What about the log book?" Donna stuck her feet on the table, emphasising her reluctance to move. "The night shift note any cameras playing up?"

"How would they know, Donna? It was dark until a little while ago."

Connor put on a pair of glasses, hauled the log book onto his lap and opened it. The zoo operated a skeleton crew at night, a handful of staff on call in case there was a break in, or one of the animals got sick.

"This is bizarre."

He flicked through the pages.

"There night staff didn't sign out." He removed the glasses again, his frown deepening. "Not one of them."

He took out his mobile and dialled.

"I bet the lazy buggers were partying." Sighing, Donna got to her feet and fastened her jacket. "They're probably still here, sleeping it off in their quarters."

"Maybe." Conner had the phone to his ear. "All I'm getting is answer messages. I can't raise them on the walkie-talkies either."

"That is *my* packet of Custard Creams." Donna glared at the others. "If I come back and even *one* is missing, I will personally feed the culprit to an alligator."

The rest of the keepers nodded agreeably, ready to help themselves to the biscuits once she was gone.

"Take one of the tranquilliser guns," Connor advised, scratching his stomach.

"What the hell for? Enclosure four is empty for cleaning."

"Because I've never seen all the cameras go down in one place at once." He began to switch on the rest of the monitors. "What if animal activists are hiding in there?"

"I'm allowed to shoot them?"

"Only in the bum. Otherwise we'll get sued."

"You are paranoid on so many levels, Con."

But Connor wasn't listening. He stood bolt upright, face twisted in disbelief.

"There are two kids in the zebra enclosure."

"They must have come over the wall," Donna said. "The zoo only opened five minutes ago. They couldn't have got to the other end that fast."

"Dammit!" One of the keepers pulled himself out of an armchair. "I better go rescue them before somebody gets kicked in the head."

"Yeah, we wouldn't want to get sued," another winked. "Would we, Con?"

Connor was finding it difficult to breathe. He sat down heavily before his legs gave way.

"Looks like one of them is already dead."

"*What*?"

The keepers leapt to their feet, knocking over the coffee table. They crowded round their supervisor, staring in horror at the screen, all speaking at the same time.

"What the hell are the zebras doing? They got the other kid trapped in a tree."

"My God, the gazelles must have *trampled* him."

"They can't have. They're scared of their own shadows!"

"What did those idiots *do* to them?"

"Get over there!" Connor shouted, wiping sweat from his brow. "Grab tranquilliser rifles and take the Land Rover with the tourist trailer hitched to it."

"All of us?"

"Everyone else is doing judge duty on that stupid bravery award!" The supervisor shooed them away, his voice rising in pitch. "You want another dead body lying out there? GO!"

The keepers pulled guns from the wall rack and bolted out of the door. Connor heard an engine start outside and pull away. He grabbed the wall phone next to his console and dialled.

"Hello. This is Edinburgh Zoo.... I need an ambulance... The emergency? I got a boy trampled to death by a bunch of gazelles."

His face reddened.

"No, I have NOT been drinking! Yes, I'll hold."

The door quietly opened and a figure slid in. It picked up a tranquilliser gun from the table and cocked it. Hearing the click, Connor whirled round.

"What the *hell*?"

The intruder fired.

The dart hit Connor in the chest, piercing his heart. The astonished man staggered backwards, colliding with the bank of screens, smashing one with his elbow. Body convulsing, he sank to his knees and pitched forwards onto the carpet.

The trespasser nudged Conner with one foot to make sure the man was dead. He picked up a keeper's hat from the table and placed it on his own head. Opened the window and gave a low whistle.

Then he locked the door again, sat down on the controller's chair and began to study the monitors.

-5-

A podium and microphone had been set up at one end of the marquee. Mondo, Akilan, Oakley and Julianne had managed to get seats together on the other side, near the entrance. Facing them were more competitors. Julianne was next to a small, willowy girl, dressed entirely in black, down to the lace fingerless gloves encasing her hands. Silver studs adorned her eyebrows and she had a pierced lip. Her tag said DAX MARTIN.

"Check *her* out, Mondo." Oakley leaned over and whispered to his gothic breakfast companion. "It's your evil twin."

"That's a devil in a dress, all right," Mondo hissed back. "I'd be drooling if I wasn't too cool to show emotion."

Akilan sat across from a tall, broad shouldered teenager, attired in a blazer as immaculate as his own.

"Akilan, is it?" the boy said in a deep plummy voice, reading the tag on his neighbour's head. "Excellent product placement, by the way."

He reached across the table. "Name's Andrew Worthington."

Akilan shook the proffered hand warmly.

31

"A pleasure to meet someone else wearing a tie. These are my scruffy new friends, Joolz, Mondo and Oakley." He glanced at Dax. "I have not yet made the vampire's acquaintance."

Dax pursed her lips

"This is Man-Bok." Andrew was seated next to an Asian boy, dressed in a muscle T-shirt and jeans. "I'm hoping he'll teach me some martial arts."

"I'm South Korean," his neighbour grunted. "Not sodding Jackie Chan."

Andrew guffawed if this was the funniest thing he had ever heard.

"Racist git," Dax whispered to Joolz. "Bet he'd rather be hunting animals than looking at them."

"Check out the size of his chin," Joolz sniggered. "He looks Mr Punch with a curly perm."

"All right." Oakley nudged Mondo. "I'm in love. With *both* those honeys."

"Hey, girls?" Mondo pushed up the table with one hand. "What animals are totally horny and sitting opposite you?"

The boys smiled brightly.

Dax gave a resigned sigh and Julianne hid a laugh behind one hand.

The Land Rover pulled up at the gate of the zebra paddock, its long trailer filled with keepers. Bangles was still in the tree, waving frantically.

As expected, the zebras and gazelles fled as soon as the keepers marched in. They bunched together at the farthest end of their enclosure, skittish and afraid, as staff helped the boy from the branches.

"I'll take the kid." Donna put her arm around Bangles and led him away. "You lot get his pal's body and see what's up with the animals."

"Don't go near dem critters," Bangles pleaded. "Dose things be dangerous!"

"They're herbivores, son," one man said. "They only eat grass."

"They didn't want to *eat* Rerun. They was out to butcher him."

"I'm sorry but you must have spooked them and driven them towards your mate," one man said. "If they'd seen him in time, they would have swerved. All he had to do was wave his arms."

"Not the time for recriminations, huh?" Donna led the boy away. "The kid's traumatised enough without you blaming him."

"Lady, those monsters be faking. They killed my cuz on purpose, I swear." Bangles was still protesting as Donna bundled him into the trailer. "Look! You left all the guns in here. You gots to arm yourselves!"

Something in his voice made Donna hesitate. The rest of the keepers were halfway across the giant paddock.

"Are you sure you weren't chasing them? I won't be angry, I promise."

"No! Dey was chasin us!" Bangles swallowed hard. "I gots a good look at em when I was in that tree and they aint normal. What kind of crazy antelope has six horns?"

"There's no need to make things up," Donna scolded. "I told you I wouldn't be angry."

Bangles picked up a pair of binoculars from the trailer and handed them to her.

"I been called a lot of things, but I aint no liar," he said coldly. "Check it."

Donna peered through the binoculars. She adjusted the focus and gave a start.

"Jesus!" She grabbed a couple of tranc guns and leapt over the side, her ample waist jiggling as she hit the ground. "Stay here!"

She ran towards her companions as fast as her robust frame would allow.

"Get back!" she screamed. "They're not our animals. They *can't* be!"

As if on cue, the beasts turned and charged.

The keepers turned and raced back, stumbling through the mud. But they were too slow and far from the gate. The group was dropped and trampled like rag dolls before they had gotten fifty yards.

Donna stood her ground, firing round after round at the approaching stampede until she was swept way. Bangles lay in the trailer, arms over his head as a tide of heaving flesh thundered past on either side. Then they were gone, leaving only churned up earth and shattered bodies.

Bangles sat up.

"I am *so* outta here."

He climbed down from the trailer and trotted towards the rope ladder. Then he stopped and looked at his watch.

It was past opening time.

"There be peeps coming into the zoo now, wid li'l kids," he muttered to himself. "An I aint no coward."

He took a deep breath and started back towards the Land Rover.

"I gots to warn them."

-6-

Ryan Forrester and Tyler Ogston strolled passed rows of empty cages, intent on a spot of thieving. Both teenagers wore gleaming white tracksuits and baseball caps pulled down over their eyes.

"Why did we have tae arrive so early?" Tyler yawned loudly. "We must have been the first people here."

Six feet two with a lumbering gait, his huge stature made him look far older than his fifteen years.

"I should still be in mah kip. The animals are no even awake."

"I told you already, eh?" Ryan was a foot shorter than his companion, thin and pale with deep-set eyes. "The mums and dads get dragged out here first thing in the morning by their kiddies, an they can't see straight until they've had a couple of cappuccinos."

"I remember now." Tyler nodded. "So, they're no on the ball."

"Absolutely, big man." Ryan pulled a cigarette from behind his ear and lit it. "The bairns start stickin their fingers into the penguin enclosure and get a wee peck for their trouble. That's them bawling their heads off. The parents rush over to kiss it better."

"And leave their bags on the bench." Tyler picked up the thread. "So we nip right over."

"Exactamundo! We're away with a purse while they're givin the poor wee mite a tellin off. Be an hour before they even miss the cash. We can do that aw day."

"Sound! Let's go see the tiger." Tyler pulled a pamphlet from his pocket. "Says here it's called Sheridan and it's the biggest one in captivity anywhere in the world. Brilliant!"

"What part of getting started early didnae sink in?" Ryan sighed. "We're no here on a bloody sightseeing trip."

"I paid £16.50 entrance fee," Tyler protested. "For that price I should get to take one of the bloody animals hame."

"But if we steal enough wallets, we'll *make* much more money than we spent."

"£16.50. That's daylight robbery." Tyler folded his arms. "You should get breakfast included for that."

"But we're gonna *end up* with much more than... Oh, never mind. Let's take a quick detour an see the tiger."

"That's OK." Tyler stopped and tapped his friend's arm. "I've spotted him already."

"Eh?" Ryan was idly poking a stick through the nearest mesh barrier, looking for the occupant. "We're no near its enclosure."

"This is as close as I want tae be." Tyler turned his friend round.

A big cat was loping down the path a mere twenty yards away. It turned a corner and vanished down another avenue.

"No way!" Ryan sprinted over to a refreshments hut and thumped on the counter. "Did you *see* that, pal?"

The white faced vendor nodded silently. He opened the door and sprinted in the opposite direction without a backwards glance.

"Cheerio then!" Ryan beckoned to his friend. "Ty! In here. Pronto."

He held the hut door open until Tyler was inside, slammed it closed and pulled down the shutters. The two boys sank to the floor, breathing heavily.

"You want to take *him* home, man?" Ryan spluttered. "You paid £16.50, after all."

"Are we safe?" Tyler checked the shutters. "When I said breakfast should be included, I didnae mean me."

"Safer than oot there, I bet."

"I'll have a hot dog then. I'm starving." Tyler grabbed a sausage and took a bite. "Should we not warn people about this, though?"

"I don't think a massive pussy on the loose is gonna go unnoticed for more than a few minutes," Ryan countered. "In fact, I can hear screamin."

"Fair enough." Tyler giggled. "Massive pussy! That's funny."

"I should be on TV, eh?" The smaller boy stroked his chin thoughtfully. "They're gonna have to evacuate the zoo now. Folk will be fleeing about like headless chickens an leaving aw their stuff behind."

"Sweet." Tyler caught on immediately. "The staff will have to abandon their cash registers, an all."

"Aye. The polis and keepers will round up that cat quick enough, but it's bound tae keep them busy for a wee while."

"We can pinch what we like while they're doin it." Tyler opened the cash register and scooped out a handful of £20 notes. "We're *so* onto a winner, man."

"Got that right." Ryan snatched the wad of cash from his companion and stuffed it in his pocket. "Let's give it ten minutes an see what else we can nab."

"Hey Ryan." Tyler took another hot dog from the rack and bit into it. "There's two tigers walking down the high street. An one says to the other…

Wow. There's no many people around for a Bank Monday holiday."

"Haw!" Ryan almost choked on his breakfast.

"Boys and girls, it's almost time to announce the winners." The zoo director suddenly appeared at his podium. "But first I'm going to get all the contestants up to say a couple of words about themselves. Not at the same time of course."

He smiled broadly at his own joke and a few adults tittered politely.

"Shame," Oakley grunted. "That'd speed things up. Make the ceremony a whole lot funnier too."

From farther up the zoo there was a burst of shrieking, followed by a man yelling.

"Well *someone's* having fun out there." The director cupped a hand behind his ear. "Never mind, we'll be joining them soon. Let's have you on first, dear."

He indicated to a freckled, redhead in the front row. "Don't be shy."

The girl, wearing a puffy green jacket that dwarfed her, stepped self-consciously up to the microphone.

"I'm called Sammy McLaren," she stammered. "I'm pleased to be here because I... eh... really like animals. I want to study zoology at university when I leave school."

A dark shadow flitted over the top of the marquee and the zoo director glanced up. Sammy quickly backed down from the podium while he was distracted. A tall athletic girl with pigtails and a long angular face stepped confidently into her place.

"My name's Liberty Bell," she announced loudly. "My parents had a weird sense of humour."

"Christ, this is bloody torture," Oakley moaned. "Make 'em stop."

Another shadow, larger this time, slid along the side of the canvass.

"What's that smell?" Joolz screwed up her nose.

"Wasn't me!" Andrew guffawed. "Can't speak for Man-Bok."

"You just did, yeah?" Dax said. "Again."

The audience could hear a rumbling noise now, like distant thunder.

"I'm an athlete," Liberty continued, raising her voice. "I'm here because I was out jogging when an old guy keeled over in front of me, so I gave him the kiss of life."

She scratched her cheek awkwardly.

"Turned out he was just drunk…"

There was a harsh yapping from right outside and the sound of tent ropes snapping. The top of the marquee sagged alarmingly.

Then the ropes on the other side slackened too - and the whole structure began to collapse. Pupils and teachers leapt to their feet, mouths open.

"This way!" Julianne was the first to react, grabbing Dax by the arm and pulling her through the marquee entrance. As the roof buckled and sank, the others at the end table followed suit. Oakley, last out, glanced back as he stooped through the crumpling gap.

Teachers and pupils surged towards him, elbowing each other out of the way and scrambling over tables. Plastic cups of lemonade and folding chairs were knocked flying, as the occupants clawed at each other in their efforts to escape. He saw Liberty Bell and Sammy McLaren squeeze through the exit at the other end of the marquee, as the canvas reached the heads of the desperate crowd and enveloped them.

Then he was out and blinking in the sunlight. Behind him, the tent was a vast white pond filled with writhing shapes, like some macabre, living bubble wrap.

Ten feet away stood a group of huge hyenas, the fur on their backs bristling and ruffling in the wind. One held a frayed length of tent rope in its slavering jaws. Oakley's newfound friends were backing slowly away, clutching each other.

The rumbling noise had now reached a deafening pitch. The lead hyena glanced in the direction of the sound and bounded sideways, followed by the rest of the pack.

Oakley spun round.

A heaving throng of gazelles, zebras, bison and wildebeests rounded the corner at a gallop, heading straight for him. The boy stumbled backwards and almost fell.

"This way!"

Liberty and Sammy were beckoning from the open doorway of the manse.

"Mondo! Joolz! The rest of you!" Oakley regained his balance and ran towards the girls. "In here!"

The others raced after him, reaching the stone building and pressing themselves against the wall, watching the herd sweep over the struggling expanse of the collapsed marquee. Dax turned her head into Joolz's shoulder and Man-Bok crossed himself as dozens of gigantic beasts ground the tent into a pulp.

Then they were gone, heading downhill towards the zoo entrance.

The marquee was a shapeless, mashed lump, an enormous red stain spreading across the dirty surface. Nothing moved underneath, though two or three broken and bloodied limbs poked up from rents made by the animal's hooves.

Andrew leaned over and threw up in the nearest rose bush. Sammy was sobbing uncontrollably and Mondo sank to his knees, hands clasped in prayer.

"This cannot be happening." Akilan stammered to nobody in particular. "This CAN NOT be happening."

Suddenly the hyenas were back, giggling fiendishly and loping towards them.

"Get in the manse," Liberty commanded, and the others piled inside. The tall girl slammed the stout door shut on the snapping jaws and leaned against it.

"Are we safe?" Mondo glanced apprehensively around.

"For the moment." Man-Bok studied the windows. They were old-fashioned and sturdy – small panes of glass divided by iron lattices. "Nothing big can get in."

He didn't sound convinced.

The children sat on the floor silently. What they had seen was too ghastly to talk about.

Akilan pulled the sticky name tag from his forehead and crumpled it into a ball.

"Know what?" Oakley tore off his badge too.

"I don't want a free pass to the zoo after all."

-8-

"Damn! There's a girl on top of an ice cream van." Sammy was peering out of the manse window. "The hyenas have surrounded her."

The others rushed over.

"What the hell is she doing up *there*?"

"I doubt she's trying to buy a Cornetto." Oakley wiped at the greasy pane.

"I talked to her earlier, yeah?" Dax said. "Her name's Siobhan Mills and she's covering the event for her blog. Saw her go out to make a phone call a few minutes before the tent collapsed."

"She's got the story of all time now. If she lives."

"She's giving it a good go."

The girl, dressed in a mini skirt and fur jacket was perched on top of the van, clutching a spade. Every time a hyena leapt up, she swung the implement at it and knocked the creature back.

"We have to help her," Joolz said decisively.

"Why?" Mondo threw his hands up in protest. "The police must be on their way and I don't think the hyenas can reach her."

"You sure about that?"

The creatures stopped leaping around the van and began tearing chunks out of the wheels, the massive jaws sinking into the rubber and slathering the black surface with drool. The van lurched to one side as the tires deflated and the girl fell flat on her back, almost sliding off the top. The beasts attacked the wheels with renewed vigour.

"Right!" Joolz stepped back from the window. "I'm going out and draw them away. How fast do you think a hyena can run?"

"Do any of us *look* like David Attenborough?"

"About 40 miles an hour," Sammy said quietly. "Humans are lucky to reach 25."

"If they get the wheels off," Dax urged. "The whole van will tip over."

"They shouldn't be able to." Sammy hesitated. "But these hyenas are different from normal."

"How do you mean?"

"It sounds dumb but they're much bigger than they should be. And those jaws are like steel clamps."

"It's only twenty yards to the nearest fence. I can be up that and over the top before they get to me." Joolz tugged off her coat. "I'll draw them away. You open the window and shout for that Siobhan girl to head for the manse."

"Don't be silly. You can't go." Andrew loosened his tie. "I'll do it."

"I can't go? Why? Because I'm female?"

"Eh… Yes, actually."

"Can the debate, you two. I'm the athlete here." Liberty elbowed Andrew out of the way and strode purposefully towards the door. "Chin? You look like you work out by lifting wads of cash. I don't think removing that tie will make you any lighter."

"They're trying to bite through the axle, guys," Dax cautioned, as the creatures began to wriggle under the van. "Looks like they might actually do it."

Liberty eased the door open and peered out. Took a deep breath. Hesitated.

"I don't know…"

Joolz brushed past her and took off for the fence, legs a blur. The girl's arms pumped and dark curls streamed behind her. The others watched in stunned silence.

She was halfway to the fence before the hyenas spotted her. Then, as one, they turned and bounded after the sprinting figure. Dax pushed open the window.

"You on the van!" she screamed. "Yeah, you! Get over here now!"

Siobhan didn't need a second invitation. She leapt down and raced towards the manse, breath erupting in terrified spurts. Reaching the doorway, she threw herself inside as Joolz approached her destination, a mere ten feet in front of the drooling animals.

The teenagers gave a cheer as she hit the fence and began to climb.

"She's going to make it!" Oakley punched the air.

Joolz went up five feet, then ten. Too high for the beasts to jump. She reached the top of the barrier and straddled it, grinning and raising her hands in a victory salute.

The eagle came from nowhere.

Wings folded, a streak of brown materialised out of the sky. It raked the top of the girl's head with its talons, before soaring off again. Joolz teetered on top of the fence, arms still raised, a line of crimson trickling down her face. Then she toppled forwards and plummeted, head first, into the snarling pack.

Liberty closed the door to drown out the sound of crunching bone and tearing tissue.

The teenage reporter sat up, nursing her shoulder.

"I lost my dictaphone!" She patted herself down. "I just recorded an interview with some girl called Rosie Wylie. She was here as a finalist."

"Why the hell does *that* matter?"

"Because now they're her last words."

She looked at the teenagers' shocked faces.

"What happened to the girl who ran past me? That was pretty awesome. Is she all right? What's her name?"

Akilan sank to the floor, staring miserably up at the ceiling.

"No comment."

-9-

The teenagers were cried out. Now they sat silently in a circle, considering their situation. Siobhan had a mobile pressed to her ear. Her long fingernails were painted bright green with little white spots.

"I've called 999 but I can't get through," she said. "That's a bit odd, isn't it?

"I'm not surprised," Mondo grunted. "Their lines must be ringing off the hook."

"We should phone our parents and let them know we're alive." Akilan got up and began studying the room. "May I use your mobile, Siobhan?"

"Where's yours?"

"The teachers took them," Dax snorted. "Didn't want us getting distracted from the wonders of nature, yeah?"

"They've certainly got our full attention now," Andrew added sourly. "*Can* we borrow your phone? The parentals will be freaking out when they hear the news."

"And I gotta put this on Facebook." Oakley joined in. "Will Oakley is likely to get eaten today."

"*That* was tasteless."

"So you won't press Like?"

"I've been calling my parents and my pals too. I even called my gran and I never talk to her, except on my birthday." Siobhan shook the device. "Maybe it's bust. I just get a weird whistling noise."

"The nearest cell tower was on the hill at the top of the zoo. Saw it a little while ago." Dax was looking out of the window again. "Only... it's not there anymore."

"Oh, c'mon," Andrew snorted. "No creature could knock that over."

"A hippo or rhino might," Sammy said. "Especially if it was bigger and stronger than before."

"What are you suggesting?" Andrew raised an eyebrow. "The animals have taken up body building?"

"I was going to be a zoologist, remember?" Sammy snapped back. "Those hyenas were almost twice normal size."

"Whatever." Mondo shuffled over to Siobhan. "Can I at least try to call my mum and dad? Please?"

"If this is the only mobile, I'm not letting the battery run down," Siobhan put the phone back in her pocket, away from the hungry eyes of her companions. "It's only half charged and I need to record what's going on. It's *my* scoop. This story is huge and I'm right in the middle of it."

The others glared at her.

"What?" She stared back. "I'm a reporter. I mean, it's only a blog right now but this will send me stratospheric!"

"A girl *died* saving you," Oakley hissed.

"You think I don't know that?" Siobhan went red. "I can't bring her back but at least I can tell my readers what she did. Besides, I'll have to keep trying to reach emergency services, won't I? Tell the police where we are."

"Put it on silent, then." Sammy pulled at her lip. "Animals are attracted by sudden noises. Like a ringtone going off."

"Absolutely." Siobhan pressed a button on the side of her mobile and quickly tucked it away again. "There. I've got it on vibrate. just in case."

She looked down at her fur jacket.

"You think I should take this off? The animals might think I'm one of them. Like camouflage, you know? Or... maybe it'll just annoy them. What do you think?"

"That you don't need the coat to be annoying?"

"I'll leave it behind."

Man-Bok strode to a door at the other side of the room and opened it a crack. On the other side was the hallway of the manse. An elegant staircase led to the first floor and large bay windows looked out onto various empty enclosures and paddocks.

Pressed against the glass were the hyenas, mucus from their jaws lathering the panes. They were looking right at him.

"Guys?" he hissed. "You'll want to get ready to run. Trust me."

He peered through the slit again. Behind the hyenas, two giraffes had appeared. A dozen pairs of malevolent eyes fastened on the Korean.

"Up the stairs!" The boy threw the door open. "They've got reinforcements!"

The teenagers were on their feet in an instant and barrelling out of the room. They skidded across the hall, sliding on the polished floor, then pounded up the staircase. The giraffes lowered their heads and butted the plate glass as the group reached the first floor. The pane gave way in an avalanche of iridescent flakes.

The giraffes withdrew their heads, shattered shards barely scratching the toughened hides. Three hyenas leapt through the gap and headed up the staircase in pursuit.

The humans surged into an oak beamed dining room, obviously used for expensive functions. Andrew slammed the door behind them and began piling chairs against it.

"Stupid thing is made of plywood," he complained. "Bloody shoddy workmanship."

The teenagers took in their surroundings properly for the first time. The dining room was decorated in a Victorian style, with a large central table and velvet curtains pinned back from the windows.

"Look at the walls!" Mondo cried.

Ornate mahogany panels were adorned with stuffed animal heads and crossed swords behind metal studded leather shields.

"Grab a weapon." Liberty hauled a sabre from its fastening and ran her thumb down the blade. "They're real and they're sharp!"

"Save me the Epee." Andrew was still barricading the door. Siobhan and Man-Bok, ran to help him. "That's the narrow one over the mantelpiece."

"Great. I'm trapped in here with Zorro." Oakley wrenched a shield from the wall and was wrestling with a sword when Dax tapped him on the shoulder.

"Wouldn't you rather have one of them, yeah?" She pointed with a black gloved hand.

"Totally." Oakley gawped. At the other end of the room stood two ornamental suits of armour, each clutching a halberd – a vicious combination of spear with an axe blade near the tip. "Those are proper!"

Ignoring the battle to shore up the splintering door, the pair ran towards the armour, Oakley hefting his shield over one shoulder. As they passed the dining room window, Dax caught a glimpse of looming yellow out of the corner of her eye.

"Duck!" she yelled, throwing herself forwards and scrabbling across the panelled floor.

"Eh? A *duck* isn't going to hurt me…"

"No! *Duck*!"

The giraffe thrust its head through the upper-story window in an explosion of shattered glass. The head was wider and broader than in any pictures the children had ever seen and topped with two sharp prongs, rather than the blunt nubs the creatures normally sported.

Oakley bent double as the animal's molars bit into the shield, lifting the boy from the ground, then slamming him back down.

The teenager landed with a grunt, instinctively swinging the shield round. The animal let go and slammed its pointed horns into the studded leather. The impact drove what little breath was left from Oakley's body, and he kicked out desperately, trying to push the creature away. Brick like teeth fastened on his jeans and the giraffe reared up, trying to yank the boy towards the window. Oakley was wrenched into the air, dangling upside down, the shield still impaled on the creature's horns.

Dax came streaking back, halberd clutched in front of her. Running at full tilt, the girl thrust her weapon into the giraffe's neck with all the force her slim frame could muster.

The halberd was sharp too. The point sliced straight through the toughened hide and emerged from the other side, dripping with blood.

The creature let go of Oakley and slammed his head sideways into Dax, eyes rolling. The boy slid under the table as his saviour was thrown across the polished top by the force of the blow. The giraffe tried to retreat but the halberd was wider than the window. It slammed into the walls on either side, trapping the animal.

The teenagers circled round the creature warily, unsure of what to do. Only Siobhan and Andrew remained at the door, still piling furniture in front.

Liberty made for the second suit of armour. The giraffe lunged forwards again, snapping at the girl. She deftly skipped out of the way and reached the other end without breaking her stride.

"Mum bought me these jeans from Harvey Nicks," Oakley complained from safely under the table. "Now I look like I've wet myself."

"Wouldn't blame you." Liberty grabbed the second halberd and came running back. She repeated Dax's actions, slamming the weapon into the giraffe's neck with a loud grunt. It, too, burst out the other side.

The beast gave a low moan and its lashes fluttered closed, almost coquettishly. The long mottled neck slid out the window until the halberds, once again, caught on the window frame. The triangular head sagged and went limp.

"That's our way out." Liberty wiped sweaty hands down her tunic. "We can go through the window and climb down its neck."

"You have *got* to be kidding me!" Mondo had squeezed himself into a cupboard and was trying to close the door.

"Hurry up chaps!" Andrew had his broad back against the chairs, trying to keep them together. "These toothy buggers are munching the door to pieces."

As he spoke a huge chunk of wood was torn loose and a hyena began to force its snout through the gap. Man-Bok rushed over and thrust a sword into the muzzle. The animal retreated with a yelp.

"Good man!" Andrew roared his approval. "Good Man-Bok!"

"Let's do it, then." Dax climbed over the giraffe's motionless head and onto the neck, boots slipping on the blood soaked hide. "But this is *really* disgusting, yeah?"

She ducked out of the window and wriggled down the neck, sword held aloft.

"Watch out for the eagle," Liberty called.

"You think I'd *forgotten* it?"

One by one, the teenagers followed her, clambering up the carcass and through the shattered window. Finally, only Man-Bok, Siobhan and Andrew were left, shoring up the makeshift blockade, stabbing through the disintegrating door with their swords.

"I've lost a nail," Siobhan complained, feet splayed and pushing her back against the chairs. "The woman in the shop said they'd never break off."

"As soon as we move, these buggers will be straight through," Andrew warned. "You pair get going."

"What about you?"

"I've already let one girl die." The teenager punched at a paw wriggling through one of the many holes appearing in the door. "I'm not about to do it again."

"Let's all run." Man-Bok pulled at the larger boy's blazer. "The gods can decide who makes it."

"I'm an atheist, MB."

"Then you won't stand much of a chance. Ready?"

"Absolutely not."

"Me neither."

All three sprinted for the window.

-10-

"Time tae get going." Ryan Forrester rifled in Tyler's pocket and retrieved the leaflet he had been consulting earlier. "There's a wee map of the zoo on the back of this."

"What's the plan, Stan?" Tyler had now finished off three hot dogs.

"Here's aw the refreshment huts." Ryan jabbed a nicotine-stained finger at various points. "We'll just pop intae them on the way oot. Grab the dough as we go, eh?"

"I'm gonnae have a different flavour of ice cream at each one. With a Cadbury's flake in it."

"Knock yourself oot, fatty." Ryan slapped his friend on the stomach. "Fish suppers are on me tonight, pal. We're gonna be living it large."

He opened the hut door and peered out.

"Not a soul in sight. Sorted!"

The teenagers strolled down the incline, Ryan guiding them using the map.

The door of the next hut was open, swinging in the breeze. A few feet away a body in a red and white striped vendor's uniform lay face down on the path, a chunk missing from his side.

"I'm no liking the look of this." Tyler raised his eyebrows. "That tiger went the *other* way."

"Go grab the money." Ryan nodded towards the hut. "I'll have a shooftie around."

Tyler vanished inside. Ryan pushed his way through thick bushes bordering the path. On the other side, according to his map, was a picnic area. He emerged from the foliage and stopped in his tracks.

"Aw, this is *totally* oot of order."

The little park was strewn with corpses. The grass was rusty with dried blood and its metallic tang filled the air, mingling with the musky smell of recently departed animals. Seagulls and crows were perched on top of the remains, pulling strings of flesh from their bodies. A child's doll lay at the teenager's feet, one severed hand still attached to it.

The hairs rose on the back of the Ryan's neck, as he suddenly realised how exposed he was. The teenager turned and stumbled back the way he had come, branches lacerating his face and hands. Bursting out onto the path he yelled a warning to his companion.

"Tyler, man! Things have gone seriously tits up!"

There was no answer.

"Tyler? TYLER!"

There was a noise to his left and Ryan spun round.

The boy was heading straight for him, a large branch in his hand. His face was set in manic determination.

"What are you doin, ya tube?" Ryan crouched defensively, throwing his arms across the back of his head. "Dinnae!"

Tyler leapt onto his friend's back and launched himself into the air, swinging the bough in a powerful arc. It connected with a swooping eagle, the bird's outstretched talons only feet above Ryan's hunched form. The wood snapped with a crunch and the eagle spun sideways in an explosion of golden feathers. It sailed into one of the enclosure fences, like a doomed warplane, crashed to the ground and fluttered weakly.

Tyler strode over and slammed the jagged edge down on the bird's head. Ryan straightened up and joined in, kicking the dead eagle until it was nothing but a heap of feathers and gore.

"That'll learn you, you big beaky bampot." He stepped back and spat at the mangled corpse, then gave it one final poke with his Nikes.

"Thanks, bud." He patted his friend on the shoulder. "But this'll no make us very popular with the RSPB."

"I've gone off the idea of ice cream." Tyler wiped speckles of blood from his forehead. "I'm no very keen on the zoo, neither."

"First time in my life I've ever tried to call the polis." Ryan pulled a mobile from his pocket and dialled. "Damn! I cannae get through. There's no signal."

"An I forgot to charge mine up."

"Let's offski, then," Ryan said decisively. "After all, money's no everything."

He pulled out the map with shaking hands.

"There's a big stone building down the hill called the manse. Looks like the safest place to hole up until help arrives."

He gave an uncertain grin.

"You never know. Maybe it has a till, an all."

-11-

The teenagers slid down the giraffe's neck as if it were some shaggy fireman's pole. Mondo, then Liberty, Akilan and Oakley. Each clambered over the rump and leapt to the ground, landing next to Dax, brandishing their swords and searching for cover.

"No! Form a circle," Liberty shouted, remembering Julianne's fate. "It's our safest option."

"Besides, we cannot leave our friends." Akilan waved his weapon at Sammy, nervously inching towards them, eight feet in the air. "It would not be civilised."

Man-Bok appeared at the window and leapt onto the giraffe's neck, almost skewering Sammy with his sword.

"Where's the bloody hell's the other giraffe?" Oakley asked as Siobhan emerged from the window behind Man-Bok. "How does something that big *hide*?"

As if on cue, a mottled head appeared round the side of the manse. The teenagers bunched together, swords outstretched, forming a human porcupine.

The giraffe ignored them and loped towards its dead companion. Sammy froze, halfway to the ground, Man-Bok and Siobhan bunched behind her. Andrew appeared at the window, one sleeve torn and an oozing gash on his arm.

"That's Britain for you," he tutted, glancing down. "Queues everywhere."

"Look out!" Liberty pointed, as a hyena rose up behind him, scrabbling to get purchase on the window ledge.

Andrew twirled and expertly impaled it on his sword. The creature gave a gurgle and fell back into the dining room.

"Three years of fencing lessons." The boy waved triumphantly. "Under 18's champion at Fettes College. Look out Man-Bok!"

The second giraffe had reached them. Sammy pressed her face into its dead companion's mane as slab like teeth clamped on her mass of red hair. The giraffe pulled up and the screaming girl was lifted from her perch.

"*That* won't work twice." Man-Bok slid forwards and sliced through the air with his weapon, taking a nick out of the assailant's nose. The giraffe let Sammy go and retreated. The girl landed back on the carcass, gripping it desperately to stop herself falling.

Man-Bok wasn't so lucky. The wild swing had thrown him off kilter and he teetered for a few seconds, arms flailing. Siobhan reached out for him, too late. Unable to regain his balance, the boy slipped from the neck and plummeted onto the path. One leg crumpled under him and he gave a wail of pain.

The giraffe abandoned its attack on Sammy and turned its attention to the prone teenager.

"Get round Man-Bok!" Liberty leapt over the fallen boy and faced the mottled leviathan, sword clutched in both trembling hands.

"Come on, then!" she challenged. "Let's see how you do against someone who can fight back!"

The giraffe edged away. Liberty beckoned to her frozen companions.

"What are you waiting for?" she urged. "We won't survive if we don't help each other."

The creature reared up and lashed out with its front legs. One hoof caught Liberty square in the forehead, cracking her skull and breaking her neck with a single blow. She crumpled to the ground, the sword clattering across the concrete in a shower of sparks.

Akilan and Dax leapt forwards, screaming in rage. The giraffe retreated a few steps then reared up again, sending the teenagers scuttling back in impotent fury.

"The other hyenas are gone." Andrew peered in the window, still unaware of Liberty's fate. "I bet they're heading back down the stairs."

Oakley and Akilan whirled to face this new threat and the giraffe headed for Sammy again.

As its mouth opened for another bite at the girl, a Land Rover pulling a trailer lurched round the corner, swaying from side to side. It crashed into the creature's rear legs and the beast went down with a startled grunt.

"What's crackalackin, peeps?" A black teenager, tractor cap stuck backwards on his head, leapt out of the cab. "Don't be letting that skyscraper wid legs get up, you feel?"

The others stared at him in stunned silence.

"What? I aint speaking English or somethin?"

"Not like I ever heard," Mondo admitted.

"I'm saying whack that sucka!" Bangles pointed at the giraffe, struggling to its feet again. "Fore it ices more of you."

Dax hesitated. Then she lifted the sword above her head and charged. The others followed suit, hacking wildly at the creature until it was dead.

"Not so civilised now, eh?" Oakley rasped at Akilan, wiping his sword on his jeans.

"Indeed. I'm no longer sure I wish to be a vegetarian."

"Thanks for the help, mate." Andrew had finally reached solid ground, right behind Siobhan and Sammy. "But, any minute now, we're going to have a couple of angry hyenas on top of us."

"Everyone in a circle again!" Dax commanded. "Just like Liberty said."

The teenagers bunched into a tight group around Man-Bok, who was struggling to get up. Bangles disappeared back into the Land Rover.

The hyenas rounded the corner and bounded towards the defiant cluster. The teens clutched their swords and pressed more tightly around the Korean.

Oakley stood on Man-Bok's leg and he gave a whimper.

"Sorry, mate!"

Phut! Phut!

The lead hyena stopped dead, pawing furiously at its face. Two brightly coloured orange tufts had appeared on the snarling muzzle.

"That be *execution* style!"

Bangles was out of the car again, legs spread apart, a tranquilliser pistol in each hand. He dropped them, reached into the cab and pulled out two more, as the second hyena evaded the bristling steel of the group and headed straight for him. Bangles fired twice at point blank range, threw himself backwards into the cab and slammed the door shut. Seconds later, the creature slammed into the vehicle, lacerating the paint with its claws.

"L'il help here, huh?" The boy's muffled voice drifted mournfully out of the vehicle. "Dose doggies be all teeth."

The hyenas seemed perfectly aware that the real threat came from the human in possession of both transport and guns. While one kept up an attack on the door, the other leapt onto the Land Rover's bonnet and tried to get purchase on the window with its fangs. The engine started up and the vehicle's windscreen wipers began to swish back and forwards, as Bangles vainly attempted to distract the animal.

But the hyenas' movements were more sluggish than before. Their snarling noticeably subdued.

"The tranquilliser darts are taking effect," Sammy whispered. "They probably contain enough morphine to stun an elephant."

"Do not tempt fate," Akilan pleaded. "If an *elephant* appears, I am likely to soil myself."

"This zoo doesn't have one, thank God."

The creature on the bonnet attempted to climb over the vehicle's roof, but its legs gave way and it slid back down, rolling over the fender and bouncing off the ground. The Land Rover lurched forwards a few feet crushing the beast under its wheels.

"There's six of us and this one's half drugged." Andrew began to advance, Dax by his side. "I'm thinking now is the best odds we're going to get."

The hyena rose up weakly, fighting to stay awake. But, in its drowsy state, the beast was no match for a crowd of sword wielding teenagers. Within seconds it too was dead.

"Get Man-Bok into the trailer." Dax grabbed the boy's arms. "Looks like his ankle's badly sprained. Might even be broken, yeah?"

They lifted the teenager and placed him gently on one of the seats. The boy gritted his teeth but refused to cry out. Bangles emerged from the cab for the last time, arms full of tranc rifles.

"Dese babies be better than the pig stickers you all packing." He dumped the guns into the trailer. "I gots plenty darts left."

"Wait." Sammy grabbed his arm. "I'm not sure taking the Land Rover is a good idea."

"Are you nuts?" Mondo was already in the trailer and trying to work out how the nearest rifle worked. "It kept this guy safe."

"Bangles is my handle…" the boy squinted at the black clad teenager's badge. "Mondo. *Thass* a crazy name."

"I told the others. Animals are attracted by noise," Sammy persisted. "This thing makes a *lot* of noise."

"I don't wanna diss you, breezy."

"I think you just did."

"But I drove all the way from the top of the zoo," Bangles continued, unperturbed. "And I didn't set eyes on a single critter till I got *here*."

"We've spotted a dozen different kinds and all the cages we could see from the manse are empty." Siobhan propped Man-Bok up on the trailer seat and made him as comfortable as possible. "They should be crawling all over the place."

She looked around uncertainly.

"Where *are* they?"

-12-

Surf rolled up the rocky beach and foamed between pebbles. Overhead Storm Petrels screeched and twirled, swooping to grab unwary fish from the white-topped waves.

Archie Lord sat on a rock staring out to sea, his mood as black as the slices of shale he was skimming into the water.

Every child in Port Cresta knew the ocean was a dangerous place. Cresta was a fishing community and each family had a tale of an uncle, father or son who had perished at sea. But Archie's own short life had not been touched by such tragedy.

Until yesterday.

Yesterday a distress call had been picked up from the trawler *Willow*, caught in a lightning storm. It was short and terse.

Mayday. Mayday. The hull has been breached by an unidentified missile. We're sinking like a stone.

Not *we're taking on water.* Not *we are abandoning ship.*

We're sinking like a stone.

That was the entire transmission. Even at eleven, Archie knew what it meant. The captain hadn't time to give Willow's co-ordinates, so there was no way the crew would have managed to unfasten and lower the lifeboat.

The coastguard did all they could, but the rescue helicopters had been beaten back by gale force winds. Even the Royal Navy, on manoeuvres in the area, joined in. The residents of Port Cresta had never seen British ships in their location before but were grateful for any help they could get.

It was a lost cause. The trawler's last position was 300 hundred miles offshore, right in the heart of a major electrical storm. None of the crew were coming home.

Captain Watson. The Daniels brothers. Beardy Pete, who hung out with Archie's big brother. Ali Le Forge. Elliot Cash, who gave the boy a toffee each time they met. All gone.

Archie picked up another slab of stone and prepared to launch it at the waves. Not that the sea would care. The sea was a huge, roaring beast that ate his people.

His arm stopped in mid throw and the lump of shale dropped from his fingers.

A naked figure was emerging from the surf.

Even at that distance, Archie recognised the limping gait.

"Captain Watson?" The boy leapt down from his perch. "Captain Watson!"

He raced towards the figure, his mind whirling. Nobody could swim 300 miles in a day, even with a lifejacket. Nobody could swim 300 miles through these squalls, in freezing temperatures, right back to the place they had left.

Nobody could swim 300 miles at all.

As he drew closer, he could see there was something wrong with the captain. He was wrenching his head from side to side, clutching at his throat. Then he toppled over and began spasming, arms and legs jerking, as if he had been electrocuted.

Watson seemed bulkier than before and was a strange grey colour. His mouth opened and closed, as he gasped vainly for breath.

Archie knelt beside him, trying to come to grips with what he was seeing.

It was impossible, of course, but he knew exactly why the captain was suffocating.

On either side of his neck was a pair of gills.

The man was still clawing at his throat and the boy saw that his fingers were now webbed. The child bit his lip.

Captain Watson groaned and his eyes rolled up in his head.

The inhabitants of Port Cresta were practical people, a trait bred into them by years of hardship. And they were experts on the sea. Impossible or not, Archie instinctively knew the solution to this problem. The man needed water to breathe.

The boy rolled the prone figure over and over, like a barrel, until the waves covered him again. Captain Watson gave a gasp and his eyes opened.

They were covered in a milky film.

He pushed himself farther out until he was fully submerged. The boy followed, mesmerised, ignoring the glacial water lapping round his waist.

Watson held up a webbed hand.

Go home.

"Where are the others?" Archie asked.

The man pointed out to sea. The boy could make out five figures bobbing on the waves, like seals. Behind them a British destroyer lurked in the mist, resembling a great grey whale.

"I'll fetch my da!"

Captain Watson shook his head. He studied the boy from under the water and put a wrinkled finger to his lips.

"I understand," the child nodded. "I'll never tell."

Watson blew a cloud of bubbles and the boy laughed.

Then the captain turned and swam away to join the others.

Archie trudged back towards the town, his spirits strangely lifted.

The sailors were mermen now. At one with the sea they had fought all their lives. And he thought they only existed in stories.

He *would* never tell.

But, suddenly, anything seemed possible. Even in this harsh world.

-Part 2-

A 62kg Orang-utan short circuited electrical wires and climbed a fence using a makeshift ladder in an escape attempt from Adelaide Zoo. Curator Peter Whitehead said Karta had twisted a stick into hot wires that encircled her enclosure, short circuiting them. She then piled up more sticks and grass roots and used them to climb onto the fence.

But her run for it was short lived. After sitting on the fence for about 30 minutes, she dropped back into her enclosure.

Associated Press

-13-

The group laid Liberty and Julianne on the path, arms folded across their chests. Then they silently climbed into the trailer and took up defensive positions, clutching their weapons.

Bangles started the engine and slowly moved off. The reluctant passengers watched the girls recede into the distance.

"Anyone know what school they were from or if they had any hobbies?" Siobhan asked. "I should put it in my report. Details like that are important. Adds a bit of human interest. "

The others glared at her again.

"Take that fork." Oakley was in the passenger seat, studying a map of the zoo. "It leads to the main entrance."

"Will do." Bangles tugged on the wheel and the Land Rover bumped into a wide lane. "You Brits drive on the right side of the road, straight?"

"Stay in the middle if you like. May as well keep our options open."

"Word. I aint got a licence, anyhow."

"Do you have a mobile?" Oakley asked hopefully.

"Course. It's American, though. Don't work here."

The vehicle putted downhill, Bangles steering awkwardly around the occasional body.

"Can't we move any faster?"

"I reckon." The boy jerked his thumb backwards. "But that trailer gonna tip over if we try."

"Never mind, we're almost there." Oakley closed his eyes.

"Just let us make it out alive, God," he whispered. "I promise I'll *never* superglue my sister's lunch box shut again."

He cocked his head. "Wait a mo. I can hear gunfire."

"Wicked!" Bangles grinned. "Somebody finally be ballin up to dose critters!"

The Land Rover emerged into an open area and the boy slammed on the brakes.

"Aw, thass bugged!"

A group of uniformed policemen in Perspex masks were crouched in a circle, firing indiscriminately. Their jackets bore the logo *Armed Response Officers*.

Around them were dozens of animals. Lions. Wolves. Hunting dogs. Wild boars. Each weaving and darting as they launched their assault. Owls and falcons bombarded the beleaguered squad from above.

"We're not getting out this way," Oakley wailed. "The entrance is blocked."

In the distance, the zoo's gates were barely visible, hidden by the foliage of a fallen oak. It was lying across the top of an armoured vehicle, turret crushed like paper.

Oakley remembered Sammy's warning. If a hippo or rhino could knock over a mobile phone mast, it would make short work of a tree.

One man released a concentrated burst of automatic fire into a group of monkeys. The bullets tore through them and shattered the observation window at the bottom of the towering penguin enclosure. The animals fled in all directions.

As the teenagers watched in horror, a torrent of water dotted with black and white birds, swept the officers off their feet and scattered them like ninepins. While they lay on the ground, coughing and spluttering, the creatures returned for the kill.

"Back up!" Oakley shrieked, as foaming water lapped round the wheels.

"I don't know how to back up wid a trailer," Bangles shot back. "I be shaky backing up *without* one."

He wrenched on the steering and the Land Rover performed an excruciatingly tight turn. Oakley could hear curses from the rear, as it tipped onto two wheels and landed back on the tarmac.

"Hold up." Bangles slammed his foot on the accelerator. "I reckon dis hulled-out ride *can* go a bit faster."

The teenagers crouched behind the iron rails of the trailer, firing and reloading the tranc rifles as fast as they could. Andrew stood in the middle, swaying

alarmingly, swinging at a pair of hawks with his sword.
The vehicle began to pick up speed.

Only two of the Armed Response Unit had managed to get to their feet. They scrambled after the Land
Rover, wading sluggishly through the torrent, but the
car was moving faster than them. Man-Bok pulled himself to the front of the trailer and pounded on the
vehicle's rear window.

"Slow down!" he yelled. "We're leaving the cops
behind!"

One of the men collapsed under a swarm of lemurs.
Oakley turned in his seat.

I can't hear you, the boy mouthed. *Engine's too
loud.*

"Slow the hell DOWN!"

The last policeman put on a final sprint, splashing
through the shallows and reaching out his hand. Blood
streaked down the man's face, emphasising the whites
of his terrified eyes.

Sheridan the tiger raced from the undergrowth in a
blur of black and orange. He swept the man away in his
jaws and was gone as quickly as he came.

Did you say slow down? Oakley shook his head in-
credulously. *Why?*

"No! Speed up!" Man-Bok urged. "Speed up!"

Make up your mind! The teenager thumped Bangles
on his shoulder and the vehicle shot forwards again.

Man-Bok sank back and inspected his swollen ankle.

"Crap," he groaned. "There's no *way* I'm getting out of this in one piece."

Tyler and Ryan reached the entrance of the manse. Broken glass littered the path and Liberty and Julianne lay on their backs beside dead hyenas and giraffes.

"Poor lassies." Tyler took off his cap. "I'm getting awful scared now."

"This may no be the safest place to hide out, after all." Ryan pushed up his cap to get a better view. "I reckon we should head for the main entrance before we end up like those two."

"I dinnae think *that's* a good idea."

Ryan was taken aback. Tyler *never* questioned his leadership.

"What's on your mind, big man?"

"You've seen the size of the walls around this zoo. If I was an animal, *I'd* be heading fur the entrance too. It's the only way oot."

"Think so? Most beasties aren't aw that brainy."

"Neither am I, bud."

"Cannae argue with you there," Ryan agreed. "Let's have a look in the manse, anyways. Maybe there's a couple of bins we can hide in till this is all over."

-14-

"Did you see what just happened?" Sammy asked the others.

"Was kind of hard to miss. Though Mondo had his hands over his eyes."

"Did not!"

"The animals were attacking the police as a unit," the girl pointed out. "Even species that are mortal enemies were fighting side by side."

"I'm sure they get fed pretty regularly," Siobhan mused. "And they're in captivity. Maybe they don't know they're meant to be eating each other."

"They might just be defending their territory," Dax agreed. "It *is* their home, yeah?"

"Oh sure," Andrew guffawed. "After this, they'll go to the zoo café and have a few Mochaccinos to celebrate."

"Herd animals work together, yes," Sammy persisted. "Different species rarely do. That lot were *co-ordinated*. And a lot of them looked different too." She bit her lip. "Bigger. More horns. More teeth. How can that *be*?"

The Land Rover chugged to a halt.

"Now what?" Dax leapt out and approached the driver's side. "Why have we stopped?"

"Nothing's following us anymore." Oakley leaned across Bangles and rolled down the window. "But we don't know where to go."

"Where exactly *are* we heading?" Mondo asked the occupants of the trailer, fighting to keep the hysteria out of his voice. "Don't bloody well hang around thinking it over!"

"The learning centre," Sammy replied, without hesitation. "After the Manse it's the most solid building in the zoo. They do lectures there, so it has rooms without windows."

"You seem to know a lot about this place."

"I already have a season pass," the girl admitted miserably. "Though I'm seriously thinking of giving up my membership."

The Land Rover headed for the learning centre, Sammy pointing the way. In the trailer, the occupants crouched, trancs at the ready. All except Andrew, who leaned over the side and vomited again. He wiped his mouth and crawled across to Man-Bok.

"Apologies if I was a bit insulting to you earlier." He dabbed his lips with a spotless handkerchief.

"Not the main thing on my mind," the boy waved a hand in front of his face. "Phew. You sure throw up a lot."

"Must have been the sandwiches I had for breakfast." Andrew leaned back and rested his head against the trailer's metal bulwark. "You shouldn't have given me yours."

"I didn't. You ate it when I wasn't looking."

"Sorry about that, as well." Andrew sat up and plunged his sword into the wooden seat, prising loose two of the thin planks. He pulled off his tie and fastened makeshift splints to the Korean's injured leg.

"There." He gave the tie one last tug. "Now you can run the hundred metres."

"In an hour and a half."

"Then let's hope you get attacked by a tortoise," the teenager smiled wanly. "There's probably one plodding after us somewhere."

The Land Rover stopped again.

"What is it *this* time?" Dax yelled.

"Keep your voice down," Mondo hissed.

"There be youngs in our way," Bangles shouted back.

The teenagers stood and peered over the top of the vehicle.

In the middle of the path was a pram. Standing a few yards away, a boy shuffled from foot to foot, his thumb stuck out like a diminutive hitcher. He couldn't have been older than seven and was carrying a large camouflaged rucksack. In his hand, he clutched a paper bag.

"I'll get him." Siobhan jumped out of the trailer, Akilan close behind. "I'm good with kids. I've got two cousins I take to the park. They don't like me much but I get paid for it."

She scooped the child up and winked at him.

"Lions and tigers and bears, oh my!" She tried to inject some levity into her voice. "Not a place for a little guy. Hey, that rhymes, doesn't it?"

"You probably scarin him more than dose critters." Bangles leaned out of the window. "You like some crazy auntie spoutin five kinds of nonsense."

But the boy threw scrawny arms round Siobhan's neck and buried his head in the girl's shoulder.

"What's your name, sweetie?" She carried him back to the transportation and put him on a seat. "Why are you on your own?"

"I'm Frankie." The child said forlornly. "I can't find my classmates. I went behind a bush for a pee. When I came out they were gone."

Akilan approached the buggy.

"The covers are moving!" he shouted. "The baby is still alive!"

"If the animals are killing everything that moves?" Sammy wondered out loud. "Why would they leave a baby alone?"

"Akilan, NO!" Oakley bellowed. "Get *away* from there!"

The boy threw back the blanket and reached out

"Oh... crud."

From the interior of the pram, a snake rose up and struck with lighting speed. Akilan jerked back, clutching his neck. Turning, he staggered towards the trailer. After a few yards, the boy's legs gave way and he sprawled across the gravel.

Oakley flung open the cab door and raced over to him, sliding to a stop and cradling the boy's head in his arms.

"I can't *die*," Akilan said feebly. "I'm going to get a bravery medal and a mention in the newspaper."

"You'll be fine. S'only a little snake."

"Ah, good." The teenager let out a long sigh and closed his eyes. "I need to be around and make sure they spell my name right."

"I'll make certain of it." Siobhan was clicking the camera on her phone. "Right under your picture on the front page, eh? Everyone will see what a wonderful guy you are."

"That would be... nice..."

"I don't know CPR," Oakley wailed. "Somebody do something! He's stopped breathing!"

"That's a Black Mamba. One of the deadliest snakes in the world." Sammy shook her head. "He's already gone."

Andrew jumped out of the trailer. With a single stroke, he severed the slithering reptile's head and kicked its body into the bushes.

"Get back in the ride." Bangles beckoned to them. "Red seems to know her stuff. You can't do nothin for your bro now."

The teenagers climbed back on board, shaking with rage. Oakley shut the Land Rover door and folded his arms, tears running down his cheeks.

"Don't cry, cuz," Bangles nudged him. "Just concentrate on surviving. Think about *revenge*."

He slammed the vehicle into gear. "Pretty soon, you an me gonna do some serious carnage in *this* hood."

The Land Rover moved off again, heading for the learning centre.

"You better believe it." Oakley's face was stone.

"We're all animals now."

-15-

The little boy sat wedged between Mondo and Siobhan, clutching the oversized rucksack and paper bag on his knees. The biting wind whipped wispy brown hair across his face but he seemed too shocked to notice.

They passed a WC, door swinging in the breeze. On the wall of the outhouse was a stark message.

Save me

It was written in blood.

"What's in the rucksack, honey?" Siobhan asked, trying to keep the child's mind off the horrors he had just witnessed. "You got a packed lunch? I like peanut butter sandwiches myself. With Branston Pickles. Some people think that's disgusting but my mum never has a lot to choose from in the fridge."

"It's empty," Frankie replied bleakly. "I thought I could hide inside, but I'm too big."

"Ah." The teenager lapsed into silence.

"Well done kid," Mondo chuckled. "You finally shut motor mouth up."

"We here." Bangles parked outside the squat building and the group disembarked, weapons at the ready. Andrew helped Man-Bok down, arm around his waist.

"The doors are closed and intact," Dax said. "That's a good sign, yeah?"

Bangles crept up and tugged on the handle.

"Iss locked."

Sammy raised her hand to knock but the boy grabbed her arm.

"Hole up, Betty." He pulled her back. "You be the bomb when it come to animals and we need that egg-spertise. Don't be putting yourself in harm's way."

"The name's Sammy," she retorted angrily. "Not Betty."

"Be easy. Where I come from, Betty means a cute girl, you feel?"

"Oh." Sammy blushed. "I didn't know."

"I aint got time to give you electrocution lessons right now." Bangles put his ear to the door. "Tell you what. If we live, how about I take you for bites? You can teach me the nutty way you Brits speak."

"You really think this is an appropriate time to be chatting girls up?" Andrew was struggling up the steps with Man-Bok. "Not that she understood a word you said."

"You think there's a *bad* time?" Bangles knocked loudly on the door. "I gots to give you some schooling bout the ladies, cuz."

They heard a shuffling inside. Then silence.

"There are no creatures out here, but we're armed," Dax warned. "So let us in *right* now, or we'll shoot the bloody hinges off."

"What if the creatures are in *there*?" Mondo whispered.

"I'll make 'em wish they stayed in their cages." The girl raised her gun. "Yeah?"

They heard the door being unlocked. It opened a crack and an eye appeared.

"No animals? You sure?"

"If there was, do you think I'd be standing discussing it?"

The door swung wider and a keeper in a green uniform beckoned to them. The group entered and took in the scene at a glance.

More children sat at desks, faces ashen. They stared at the newcomers hopefully.

"Is it over?" one of them whispered.

"Fraid not," Oakley shook his head. "We're hiding, just like you."

"Holy hell," the keeper said. "How did you manage to stay alive out there?"

"We did a lot of fleeing."

"My name's Jamie Corstorphine." The man shook Dax's hand warmly. "I was getting ready for a school lecture later today when all hell broke loose."

"It's still breaking loose, Mr C." Siobhan peered through the blinds. "Some cops tried to get in, but they've been slaughtered. Now the entrance is blocked and there are animals are gathered all round it. We can't get past."

"I won't insult your intelligence by pointing out how absolutely ridiculous this situation is." Jamie locked the door again. "I've seen what's happening with my own eyes."

"We've lost three so far." Mondo ran a hand through his blue streaked hair. "They were all our age."

"Shhhhh." Jamie put a finger to his lips. "Don't make my lot even more scared."

"Who are they?" Dax asked. "Where are their parents?"

"Four of them were on a school trip which turned up early. They got separated from their group and came looking for their pals." Jamie's expression left the girl in no doubt what he thought had happened to those friends.

"The big blonde kid was on a bike. He only just made it inside, cause he went back for a bag strapped to the back of it. Damned fool. Had a pack of Colobus Monkeys after him." Jamie seemed on the verge of crying. "They were trying to turn the handle, so I locked the door. I *had* to."

"Have you managed to call anyone?"

"My mobile isn't getting a signal. Same with the kid's phones."

Oakley approached the seated children, holding Frankie's hand.

"I'm Will Oakley." He patted the little boy on the head. "This is Frankie."

"I've got Jelly Babies." The child held out his paper bag. "Have one."

"Brandon Golledge." A tall boy with a shock of platinum blonde hair got up and accepted a sweet. "Thanks. I was running late and didn't even have time for Corn Flakes."

He introduced the others.

"The tall one is Sasha Sorokin. That's Kirsty Noble with the short hair. The other two are Max and Sue." He furrowed his brow.

"My bad, guys. I've forgotten your last names."

"You've got guns." Kirsty Noble eyed the weapons hungrily. "Any chance of me getting one?"

"Not much point." Oakley chucked his pistol to the girl. "I got no darts left and the others are almost out as well."

"Just holding it makes me feel better."

"We tried to make our own weapons." Sasha Sorokin reached into his desk and held up a ruler with a pair of scissors sellotaped to one end. "But this is a kid's corner, so there aren't any sharp objects."

"Political correctness gone mad," Andrew tutted. "All play areas should include a gun."

"Let's pool what we have," Dax said. "Give all the tranc darts that are left to Bangles. He found the weapons in the first place. We still have our swords, yeah."

"I've got this." Brandon pulled a penknife from his pocket. "It's a bit blunt but has a tin opener on the side."

"Somebody will be coming to save us, won't they?" Sue wailed. "We just have to wait here."

"I dunno." Oakley shook his head. "All those Armed Response Officers are dead…"

Dax kicked his ankle.

"Yeah." The boy backtracked. "Someone's sure to come get us soon."

Frankie wandered disconsolately round the room, handing out Jelly Babies.

"Sorry," Oakley wrinkled his nose. "Don't like them."

"Yes. My mummy said you should never take sweets from strangers." The boy looked dejected. "But I'm one of you now, aren't I?"

His lip trembled.

"I don't want to be left behind again."

"I didn't mean…." Oakley sighed. "OK. Give me a jelly baby."

-16-

"You've got a walkie talkie." Siobhan picked up a small device on the table and studied it. "It's pretty cheap, though, so you won't be able to pick up the police frequency. Me? I've got a CB radio in my bedroom to monitor their channels. I like to keep abreast of any potential major stories."

"She thinks she's a hot shot journalist," Mondo explained.

"If an animal gets loose, I'm supposed to radio it in to a guy called Connor in the zoo's control centre near the south wall," Jamie said. "Only he's not answering. Nobody is."

The children sat in a ring, facing each other.

"Do we just wait?" Mondo asked. "The police are bound to try again."

"What makes you think a new attempt would be any more successful?" Dax replied sourly. "They obviously can't get another vehicle through the entrance and I bet they'll think twice about going in on foot again."

"Redwood army barracks is only twenty miles away," Man-Bok interrupted. "I live near it. They'll have much better guns."

99

"The army is on manoeuvres in the highlands." Andrew shook his head. "Some big military training exercise. My mate's in the T.A. and he went too."

"The whole lot are up north?"

"Apparently. Crappy timing, eh?"

"Surely they could have gotten a fighter jet here already," Mondo said. "Those things go at supersonic speed."

"I've been thinking about that and nothing's adding up." Siobhan's brow furrowed. "This disaster must be all over the news and social media and Forth Radio and Scottish Television both have helicopters. I used to go down to their studio all the time, to see how the professionals work. Until they asked me to stop bothering them."

"Could you get to the point, Siobhan?" Man-Bok asked patiently.

"Why aren't they flying over the zoo filming the news story of the decade? And Mondo's right. Why have no army jets or police choppers arrived?"

"My dad's with the North Berwick Coast Guard." Kirsty Noble raised a hand. "He knows I was visiting the zoo this morning. I'll bet he's on his way right now."

"We're not anywhere near the sea, kid," Oakley said patiently.

"He's not a sailor. He flies a rescue helicopter."

There was a stunned silence.

"If you tune in to frequency 26MH he might even close enough for you to contact him on that radio."

The children let out a subdued cheer and Kirsty finally smiled.

"I'll have to get a few words from you later. For my blog." Siobhan fiddled with the knob on the walkie talkie and handed it to Kirsty. "Here you go."

"Mayday, Mayday." The girl pressed send. "Are you there dad? Over."

The radio crackled to life.

Kirsty! Baby! You all right?

"I'm fine! I knew you'd come! I'm here with a bunch of other kids."

I was told everyone in the zoo was dead!

"Aw, that's just fantastic!" Mondo threw up his hands.

"Where are you dad? Over."

I'm ten minutes away but there's only one area in the zoo big enough for me to land. It's called Wilson Park. Are you near it?

The girl looked at Jamie and he nodded.

"We're not too far. Over."

Go there right now. I'll pick everyone up.

"What's going on? Over."

The authorities are saying terrorists released some kind of virus in the zoo and it drove everyone crazy, even the animals. The place is quarantined in case it's infectious and the area above is a no-fly zone. Nobody is to get in or out. Radio chatter claims the army is putting together a hazmat team but I couldn't wait.

"You'll be in a lot of trouble, won't you? Over."

"You think I care, baby? There was a pause. *You're not sick, are you? Please tell me you're OK?*

"None of us are sick! I promise."

You can tell me the details once we're far enough away. Then I'll radio the authorities and tell them they're wrong. Just get to that park.

"We will. I love you. Over."

"I love you too. With all my heart. Over and out.

"That's my dad," Kirsty announced proudly.

"Now we know why the policemen were wearing respirator masks," Man-Bok said. "They're afraid there's some sort of plague loose in the zoo."

"You think we're infected?" Mondo whispered. "I feel fine."

"We don't have any disease," Sammy assured him. "Neither do the animals."

"You sure?" Oakley squinted at her. "They're certainly acting like they have rabies or something."

"I'm positive." Sammy insisted. "We've seen those creatures close up. Some have horns and teeth where they shouldn't. In the course of one night, they've mutated beyond recognition. No virus on earth, natural or man-made, could do that."

"So what caused them to change?"

"I've no idea. But it hasn't affected us, that's for sure. If it did, half of you would be growing tusks."

"Shame," Oakley grunted. "That'd come in pretty handy right about now."

"Sammy's right," Jamie agreed. "I've been around animals all my life and never seen anything like it. Anyway, what kind of terrorist would target a half empty zoo?"

"Let's save the pow-wow for later, compadres," Bangles interrupted. "We best be ghosting this joint, pronto."

-17-

"Wilson Park is between the night keeper's accommodation and the reptile house," Jamie said. "It's only a few hundred yards."

"A park sounds pretty exposed, yeah?" Dax reminded him. "Standing around outside we may attract more than Kristy's dad."

"I have keys to the night keeper's quarters. We can hide inside until the chopper arrives." The keeper snapped his fingers. "There'll be more guns and ammo too."

"Do we run or take the Land Rover?" Andrew asked.

"We'd be sitting ducks on foot."

"Right guys!" Dax clapped her hands. "We're heading out. Everybody keep their wits about them. Oakley? Would you look after Frankie?"

"He can sit on my knee in the cab."

"I be takin the wheel." Bangles' hand shot up. "Always wanted to be a getaway driver."

"I think you better leave this to an adult..." Jamie began.

Dax laid a hand on his arm.

"He's responsible for getting us the truck and guns *and* he rescued everyone." She gave Bangles a thumbs up. "He's got a cool head in a tight situation."

"For rizzle." The boy gave her a thumbs up. "I'll be gettin you to dat chopper in a hot minute."

Sammy sidled over to him.

"Sorry for being so bitchy earlier," she apologised. "I didn't even thank you for saving my life."

"You got red hair, green eyes an a ba-dink-a-dink that don't quit." Bangles doffed his cap at her. "Gotta go hard to impress *you*."

"You certainly have." Sammy gave a little curtsey. "Wait? Are you talking about my bum?"

"Bum!" Bangles threw up his hands. "I just love the way you foreign crackers speak. Where I come from, a bum sits on the street corner asking for cabbage. Eh... I mean money."

"Most people don't think I'm cute. They don't usually notice me at all."

"My guess is, thass cause you don't want em to."

"Touché."

"You speak French? Hot damn!" Bangles waggled his eyebrows roguishly. "Sides, I aint most people, you feel?"

"I feel."

"Then let's blow this popsicle stand." The boy wagged a finger at her. "Don be trying no heroics, though."

"Eh... Have you met me?"

"I'm thinkin you tougher than you look. Juss stay on point and keep your head down."

The kids began to form a line by the door. Mondo grabbed Dax as she walked past his chair.

"I don't think I can leave," he hissed.

"I'm not exactly looking forward to it myself. But it's our best chance."

"I *know* that, Dax." Sweat slicked the boy's forehead. "I'm just *so* scared."

"Mondo. You're up for a *bravery* award."

"All I did was throw a wet towel over a burning chip pan."

"I'll stick with you." The girl hunkered next to him. "Just keep it together, yeah?"

"You mean it?" Tears dripped from Mondo's long lashes. "I need you to *mean* it."

Dax stared at him for a long time. She lifted his chin and looked into the boy's bloodshot eyes.

"I'll stick with you," she repeated. "I promise."

"On my back, Man-Bok." Andrew knelt down. "We got to get to the Land Rover fast. No time for hobbling along like some pensioner."

"This makes me feel so bloody useless." The boy wrapped his arms round his companion's neck. "Do I hold your ears to steer?"

"Highly amusing, I *don't* think." Andrew stood up with a grunt. "Thank goodness you Orientals are so small."

"South Korea isn't in the Orient. And you obviously haven't met my aunt Chak."

"When this is over, feel free to introduce us. She can make me a curry."

"Don't you think we eat dogs or something equally xenophobic?"

"Man-Bok? Eating *any* kind of animal would be sweet revenge to me."

Oakley tapped Frankie on the shoulder.

"We're making a run for it," he said. "Take my hand and don't let go."

"Where we going?"

"For a ride in the big sky bird."

"You mean a helicopter?" The child regarded him evenly. "Where are we going to wait for it?"

"The night keeper's quarters."

"Oh." Frankie's grip tightened.

"You have to be brave." Oakley stroked the child's head, at a loss for how to reassure him. "I'm sure eh... God.... wouldn't let a nice little kid like you come to harm."

"I don't think God is listening, Oakley," Frankie whispered in his ear. "Satan has taken over this place."

"Whatever works for you, buddy." The boy shivered.

"But you'll need some serious counselling when we get out of here."

-18-

The group emerged from the learning centre, hurrying quickly and quietly towards the Landover. Grimy and exhausted, they moved like a small army rather than a group of abandoned and shell-shocked teens. Every sense was heightened. Each face set in resolve.

The motley group piled into the trailer and Bangles set off for Wilson Park. Oakley guided him, while Frankie held the map.

"I might juss become a cab driver when I'm older," Bangles observed, sagely. "You gets paid for sittin on you bum all day."

He sniggered to himself.

"Bum! Thass a bitchin word for bootie."

"True dat," Frankie said solemnly.

"This little dude be pickin up the way I talk!" Bangles grinned. "He a smarty-pants an no mistake."

"Are you *enjoying* this?" Oakley exploded. "We're up to our necks in corpses!"

"I seen my friend get gored to death this morning." the teenager's grin vanished and he looked coldly ahead. "I be cheezin to keep *your* spirits up."

"Oh." Oakley sounded contrite. "Sorry, Bangles."

"Iss cool. We gotta be optimistic for the tiny bro, so he got some hope goin on. Looks like you his baby daddy for now."

"Eh… Word."

"Thass more like it!"

"You wanna play I spy, Frankie?" Oakley tapped the child's head.

"No need to go overboard, cuz." Bangles pulled a face. "He say 'T' and I be thinking dat *tiger* in the hood. Crash this ride, for sure."

Man-Bok was propped up against the top of the trailer, his strapped up leg resting on a cushion. He watched the enclosures speed past, trying to ignore the pain.

He poked Andrew's hip.

"None of the enclosure fences are broken."

"That's handy." The teen was scanning the skies, having decided that bird defence was his speciality. "The zoo probably won't have much cash left for repairs, after half the population of Edinburgh *sues* them."

"You're missing the point."

"Yah. I'm a little distracted."

"The fences are all intact, Andrew. So, how did the animals get *out*?"

That got everyone's attention.

"Man-Bok's right." Siobhan turned to Jamie. "The creatures may be acting together but they couldn't possibly open the locks to their own cages. Could they?"

"Not a chance." Jamie studied the passing enclosures carefully. "Somebody with keys would have to set them free."

"So, who has keys?"

"Only the keepers. And nobody could unlock the enclosures without being spotted, not once the zoo was open." Jamie looked abashed. "It would have to be done at night or very early in the morning."

"And the other staff didn't *notice* when they got here?"

"An unlocked gate looks exactly the same as a locked one. So they went for breakfast or to judge that ceremony. Even the animals might not have realised they could get out right away."

He rubbed his chin.

"Unless..."

"Unless what?"

"Unless they deliberately waited for visitors to arrive before they emerged."

"Try and stay on planet earth, yeah?" Dax grunted

"If they're stronger and different looking, why couldn't they be smarter too? After all, the way they're acting seems so... so..." Jamie searched for the right word. "*Calculated.*"

"You think the night keepers might have some answers?"

"Hopefully, we'll find out." The man pointed to a low concrete building ahead.

"That's their quarters."

The group waited nervously while Jamie unlocked the front door and cautiously entered. Seconds later, the blinds parted and he waved to them.

"All clear."

Oakley picked Frankie up and put a hand over his eyes, as the group entered.

But there was nobody in the main room. Half-eaten sandwiches lay on the table beside empty coke bottles. On the wall was a whiteboard with a rota sketched out in red marker pen.

"There's a landline here." Oakley picked up the receiver and listened. "It's dead. I bet some creature knocked down the pole outside or bit through the wire."

"I'll write a letter of complaint to BT first thing." Andrew helped Man-Bok into a tatty chair. "I mean, what if there was a *crisis* or something?"

The children flopped down on the worn leather couches or took up position beside the windows. Jamie peered at a near empty line of hooks above the sink.

"The keys are gone." He looked shocked. "Somebody *did* unlock the cages."

He opened a cupboard and felt around the back. "But there's a secret one kept up here."

He retrieved a sliver of silver.

"It's for the arms cabinet over there. That's why it's hidden." Jamie handed the key to Oakley. "See what's inside. I'll check the sleeping quarters."

He pushed open a side door and darted inside, tranc gun held in front of him. Oakley unlocked the cabinet and began passing out weapons.

"Two more tranc guns. Plenty darts." He stopped and whistled. "There's a couple of proper rifles and a pistol."

"I'll take a rifle." Dax dropped her rapier and pushed him out of the way.

"I'd like the other one." Andrew sauntered over. "I'm rather good at…"

"Yeah, yeah. You were the under eighteen's clay pigeon champion at Poncenby snooty-boy college."

"No. I'm rather good at *archery*." The teenager eyed the rifle hopefully. "So I've got excellent hand-to-eye co-ordination."

"Which makes you deadly with a sword." Dax grabbed the remaining weapons. "I actually know how to shoot."

"*You're* a marksman? I mean woman?"

"Hundreds of hours on the X-Box. It's the same thing."

"It would be if we were fighting Sonic the Hedge-hog."

"That's Nintendo," Dax held out the pistol. "Bangles? You want this?"

"What? You think cause I'm black an come from da hood, I be all thugged?"

"You want the damned weapon or not?"

"Tool me up, babe."

"I'll take the other rifle," Siobhan said. "I've done some practise at the local range in case I ended up covering a war zone or something. Of course, I didn't expect to be in one for a few more years."

"You're unbelievable." Dax tossed her the weapon. "I can't tell if you're a deluded bimbo or the most sussed person I ever met."

For the first time, there was a hint of admiration in her voice.

"There are knives here too," Mondo was pulling open drawers in the tiny kitchen. "Every little helps."

As the children began tucking assorted blades into their belts, Jamie emerged from the side room, visibly shaking.

"Don't go in there."

"Why?" Siobhan made for the door, pulling out her phone. "It can't be anything worse than we've already seen. I need to get details for my story."

"Don't go IN there!" Jamie commanded. "It's the night keepers. They're all dead."

"What killed them?" Siobhan persisted. "The outside door is locked."

"There's an open window in the sleeping quarters."

"Did you shut it?"

"No, I fancied some fresh air," Jamie growled. "Of course I shut it."

"I'm only asking." Siobhan looked around. "Why does everyone find me so irritating? Ok. I talk a lot. But that's because I'm terrified. It's a coping mechanism, for God's sakes."

"Don't blow a gasket," Dax said gently. "I understand. We're all a bit frazzled."

"From what I could see, the night keepers were killed in their sleep." Jamie looked lost. "But I don't know what did it."

"You work here," Mondo grunted. "You must have some idea."

"Why would I? I look after the giraffes."

"Should have looked after them better, then," Oakley scoffed. "You're out of a job now."

"Can *I* take a peek?" Sammy piped up. "I'll be careful."

"I don't see the point…"

"This betty be the bees knees when it come to bougie critters." Bangles jumped to her defence. "She a walking Wikipedia. Might even know what killed the keepers."

He twirled the pistol cockily round his finger. "I'll keep her covered."

"Be *bloody* careful." Jamie half opened the door and Sammy and Bangles slipped through.

"If you see anything with more than two legs, high tail it back out."

-19-

Bangles snapped a curtain rod from above the window.

"Safety's off." He handed Sammy his gun and approached one of the beds, a tousled head sticking out of the duvet. "They be anything else snakey under those covers, get ready to cap it."

He flicked back the duvet with the broken pole and skipped away.

Sammy tried not to retch.

A man lay in a foetal position on the mattress. His face and body were red and blotchy, the exposed skin covered in small crimson lumps.

"Oh, snap." Bangles turned away in disgust. "Look like he been shootin smack and ran outta places to stick the needle."

"The wounds seem to be tiny stings or bites." Sammy leaned closer. "Some kind of insects would be my guess."

"Woah! Get back fore you find out first-hand." The boy prodded her with the stick. "No need to be a shero."

"Bangles?" Sammy whispered.

"Wassup?" The boy took up a karate stance. "You spot somethin?"

"Look at the beds." Sammy pointed. "Five in total and they've all been slept in."

"So?" Bangles shrugged.

"There are only four bodies," the girl whispered. "One of the keepers is missing."

Sammy and Bangles sat next to each other on the couch. The rest of the kids were stationed at the windows or slumped on the floor.

"I've no idea which member of staff is still alive," Jamie said. "The night shift are normally gone before I clock on. I don't know them."

"Something crazy must have happened in this zoo last night." Siobhan was in the doorway, taking pictures of the corpses on her phone. "It obviously did something weird to the animals. Could it have affected the missing keeper too?"

"I don't want to think that." Jamie picked up the thread. "But *someone* used the keys to unlock all the cages early this morning."

"Why didn't the animals kill him?"

"Maybe they did. Here's hoping, anyway."

Frankie sat down at a computer in the corner and was about to close down the window on the screen when Mondo loomed over his shoulder.

"Can I have a go?"

"I want to play Angry Birds," the child slapped him away.

"Plenty of angry birds already out there, Chuck," Oakley snorted. "I'm sure they'd *love* to play."

"This thing has internet," Mondo said excitedly. "We could contact our parents."

He squinted at the screen and tapped some keys.

"The web's down too, but there's a couple of pages on the screen. Must be the last thing the keepers were looking at."

"What is it?" Dax trotted over and read the headlines.

Rumours of cannibal children reported

<u>Port Cresta</u> Trawler Missing In the Atlantic Ocean

"Morbid bunch." She shut down the entry. "Any normal person would be looking at porn."

"What's porn?" Frankie asked.

"Never you mind."

"Let me try to get connected again." Mondo was hopping from foot to foot. "Maybe I can email my parents."

"No time." Brandon was peering through the blinds on the window.

"I can hear the chopper."

"Everyone get ready to move," Jamie said. "We need to be exposed for as short a time as possible. Safer to go in groups."

Man-Bok hoisted himself onto Andrew's back. Oakley took Frankie's hand. Siobhan gave the discarded swords to Sasha, Max and Sue. Kirsty loaded her tranc gun and pulled a fire extinguisher from the wall for good measure.

Jamie opened the door and stepped back as the descending chopper's rotors whipped up dust, leaves and crisp packets into a miniature maelstrom. It landed in the little park and a man beckoned from an open side panel.

"It's dad!" Kirsty squealed. "Told you!"

"Sasha, Brandon, Max and Sue. Go with Kirsty!" Jamie pushed them outside.

The children scurried across the grass, clutching their weapons. They climbed into the helicopter, chattering with relief, while Siobhan readied the next cluster.

"Andrew, Man-Bok, Oakley, Frankie, Mondo and Dax. You ready?"

They nodded.

"Out!"

The teenagers sprinted.

"The rest of us should elevate right now. I swear I seen a big blue butt up in dat tree." Bangles pointed. "I aint clownin. It a monkey or somethin?"

"Give me the gun!" Sammy seized the boy's pistol and fired it in the air. The teenagers halted in their tracks.

"Mandrill baboons!" She waved both hands above her head. "They've got teeth like razor blades!"

A horde of apes with brightly coloured faces dropped from the trees and loped towards the chopper. Dax did an about-face, and raced back, Mondo keeping pace with her. Andrew hobbled behind with Man-Bok hugging his neck. Oakley hesitated. The helicopter was only a few feet away.

Before he could make a decision, the chopper began to rise. Three baboons leapt through the open door and vanished into the interior. The others clung onto the wheels and pulled themselves up, swarming over the fuselage. The helicopter tilted alarmingly.

Oakley dropped his tranc gun and dived for cover, pulling Frankie off his feet. The rotor blades sliced through the air just above their heads as the helicopter levelled out and climbed again. Oakley scooped the child into his arms and vanished round the side of the reptile house, leaving the pistol behind.

Dax, Mondo, Frankie, Andrew and Man-Bok regained the safety of the keeper's quarters. The chopper rose again and hung in mid-air.

"Look!"

Brandon leapt from the helicopter and landed on the reptile house roof. He ran to the edge and jumped again, hitting the grass and rolling to break his fall.

Then he sprinted towards the keeper's quarters and flung himself through the doorway.

"Respect, bro." Bangles pulled the teenager to his feet. "You be a regular Houdini. You're imperishable!"

"Are you ok?" Sammy inspected a gash on the boy's cheek.

"They went straight for the pilot. Like they knew he was in control."

The helicopter lurched sideways as more mandrills clambered inside. Then it began to fall.

"Look out!" Dax pushed the teenagers back.

The chopper hit the reptile house roof and disintegrated.

Jamie slammed the door shut as pieces of broken metal thudded into the wall of the keeper's quarters.

"Those poor kids," he said. "Those poor bloody kids."

-20-

"I don't see any point in waiting around, yeah?" Dax went to the sink and splashed water on her face. "I say we try and get out of the zoo ourselves."

"The front way is a no-go." Andrew turned to Jamie. "Are there any other exits?"

"They'll still be locked." The keeper nodded towards the empty hooks. "And the keys for them are gone too. We could search around and try to find something to prop against the wall but it's topped with barbed wire all the way to the far side of the zoo. The wire stops at the east wall but that's quite a distance. Plus it's still high and studded with broken glass."

"Not going to work, anyway," Brandon said evenly. "I got here early and cycled past a whole bunch of stuff we could use to get over. Planks and bits of scaffolding. Even a wooden ladder."

"So what's the problem?"

"When I came back it was all gone." The boy shrugged. "It's not just the authorities who don't want anyone leaving this zoo. I hate to say it, but the animals must have moved them."

"I snuck in usin a rope," Bangles piped up. "It's way up at the top corner of the hill where dose zebras hang, an almost invisible."

"And you decided not to *mention* that fact?"

"Didn't fancy our chances of reaching it. But iss lookin more attractive by the minute."

"So?" Andrew turned to the others. "Do we go east or stay here?"

"I say we leave." Siobhan hoisted the rifle onto her shoulder. "Story's out there, after all."

"We'll take the Land Rover." Jamie's face was grey. "And run down anything that gets in our path."

"Each of you has to make your own choice," Dax said. "Me? I agree with Jamie and Siobhan."

"The army are on the way." Mondo objected. "Kirsty's dad said so."

"We don't know how long it will take them to get here," Siobhan reminded him. "Plus they'd have to come in on foot, cause now there's wreckage all over the only place where they could have landed a chopper."

"So it'll take a while," the boy said stubbornly. "This place is defendable if we all stay together."

"The animals are working together too, remember?"

"Most of them don't seem too interested in us," Mondo insisted.

"Yah, but the fraction we *have* encountered wiped out half our party." Andrew pulled on his long chin. "They're not just wild. They're absolutely furious."

"It's settled. We take the Land Rover." Jamie beckoned to Bangles. "You still want to drive, hotshot?"

"You know it."

"I think we should split up and go on foot," Sammy said. "All of us in one vehicle is too easy a target."

"Ride got us this far, Sammy." Bangles objected. "An my driving aint *that* bogus."

"Got us where exactly? We're still in the middle of the zoo." The girl refused to budge. "I'm going to try and make it on foot. I'm good at being invisible."

A look of regret slid across her face.

"Always have been."

"Guh!" Bangles tossed the Land Rover keys to Jamie and joined the girl. "Sammy been right about everything so far. I'm bouncing with her."

"You don't have to," the girl said shyly. "It's probably a stupid idea."

"Naw, Sam. Climbin into this zoo to sit on a zebra. Now, *that* was a dumb notion." The boy beamed. "This the most sensible decision I be makin all day."

"Thank you, Bangles."

"Me and Man-Bok are opting for the trailer." Andrew reached out to the Korean. "He can't walk on his own."

"No. Hand over a weapon and leave me here." The boy pushed him away. "You stand a much better chance on your own."

"How would I face your aunt Chak?" Andrew smiled bravely. "I'd be doing myself out of a decent curry."

"It *is* tasty." The Korean gave a thin smile. "So are we, apparently."

"That's the spirit, M.B." Andrew helped him to his feet. "Anyway, you still have my tie."

Man-Bok sighed.

"And I always swore I'd never wear one."

"I'm not moving." Mondo rubbed a hand across his mouth. "I can't go out there again."

Dax looked longingly at the door.

"Then I'm staying too," she said finally.

"What I said earlier? You don't have to…" Mondo picked up Sacha's ruler with the scissors fastened to the top. "Look. I'm armed."

"I don't break my promises." Dax unslung her rifle. "Anyway, I bet you're right. This is probably the safest place to be, yeah?"

"Brandon?"

"My mountain bike is lying out there." The blonde boy hoisted his precious satchel onto muscular shoulders. "I'll take that."

"Are you nuts?" Siobhan threw up her hands. "Haven't you stretched your luck to breaking point? It's a bike, not the sodding Batmobile."

"I'll make it, don't you worry." Brandon took a comb from his pocket and ran it through his hair. "Besides, I'm looking for someone."

"Could you *be* any more cryptic?"

"It's a long story and I don't have time to tell it."

There was nothing left to say.

"All rightee. Good luck everyone." Andrew tucked in his shirt. "Are we having a moment? Do we want a group hug?"

"Like I want a damned hernia." Dax held out her arms. "But today I'll make an exception."

They embraced briefly. Stepped back awkwardly.

"Let's do this."

Jamie, Andrew, Siobhan and Man-Box piled into the Land Rover. Bangles and Sammy started north up the hill, sticking close to the bushes. Brandon pulled the mountain bike upright and inspected it for damage. Mondo sat on the keepers' couch, staring at the ruler. Dax watched the others go, biting her lip.

But she had promised.

She shut the door.

None of them noticed fuel dripping from the ruined carcass of the helicopter and soaking into the gravel underneath.

-21-

"Looks like it's you and me, kid." On the other side of the reptile house, Oakley knelt by Frankie, wiping dirt from the child's face. "The monkeys might still be at the learning centre, so we better not go back."

"I dropped my Jelly Babies."

"When we escape, I'll buy you a whole tub."

"The Ape Pavilion is this way." The boy started off.

"Wait. Why would we go there?"

"The chimps' cages have roofs, so they can't climb out. My teacher, Mrs Duffy, told me."

"I'm not following."

"Shouldn't we find one and shut ourselves in?" the child replied. "Then we'd be safe till someone rescued us."

Oakley stared at him. "Holy shit. Why didn't any of us think of that?"

He took the boy's hand.

"Lead the way. Fast as your little legs can go."

Five minutes later, they reached the pavilion. Wooden doors with a cut-out silhouette of a chimpanzee marked the entrance.

"Stay behind me," Oakley cautioned. "We don't know what's in there."

As he stepped forwards, there was a low growl ahead. A cape hunting dog emerged from the shrubbery and blocked their path.

"Back up," the teenager hissed.

"Oakley," Frankie slid behind him. "Mr Duffy said those dogs hunt in packs."

As if on cue, another creature appeared on the path to their right. The teenager slowly turned.

There was a third on their left. And two on the lane behind. They drew their lips back over wrinkled muzzles and began to inch towards the pair.

"I'll take the one in front." Oakley pulled the sleeves of his sweatshirt over his hands. "When I do, run round us into the pavilion and shut the door."

"They'll kill you."

"Nah. They just want to play. Don't look back though."

The child's expression betrayed exactly what he thought of *that* explanation.

"Ready?" The teenager raised his barely covered fists.

The lead dog crouched down, belly scraping the path, preparing to pounce.

"Poochie-woochies!" a muffled voice cried behind them. "You're about to get some fucking *serious* dog trainin!"

Two suits of armour were clanking up the hill, each carrying a large sword.

The hound leapt past Oakley and raced towards the intruders, the rest of the pack at its heels. Their teeth fastened on metal, to no avail. The swords flashed in air as the assailants sliced and stabbed at the creatures.

"Nothin worse than food that winnae come out of the can," one whooped, thrusting his weapon into a snarling canine.

Within minutes, all the dogs were dead.

"Better than a slap on the nose wi a rolled up news-paper, eh?" The figure pushed up his visor. "Name's Ryan, lads. The other sardine tin is Tyler."

"How's it going?" The big teenager took off his hel-met. "Thought you could do wi a bit of help."

"I'm Oakley and this is Frankie." The boy gave a shuddering sigh of relief. "You saved our lives."

"Aw part of the service," Ryan grinned. "Where you off tae?"

"Somewhere safe." Oakley pointed to the pavilion. "Want to join us?"

"Long as it has air conditioning, pal. I'm sweatin like a pig in this get up. It doesnae fit, neither."

"Stop wandering about Frankie," Oakley warned. "Stay close to me."

"Just looking around."

"Well, don't." The boy beckoned urgently. "In case you find something that munches your tiny head off."

The pavilion was dimly lit and there was no sign of any animals. They climbed a flight of stairs, walls decorated with pictures of the great apes that had once been contained there. At the top was another level, looking down into enclosures filled with denuded trees. It too had an entrance, so visitors could get in from further up the hill.

"Let's try to make this place more secure." Oakley flipped the latch on the lock of the upper doors, then grabbed a discarded mop and shoved it through the handles. "I don't see a way to blockade the bottom door, though. Do you?"

"Let me get mah breath first." Ryan flopped down on a bench, which creaked alarmingly. "If I wanted tae cart round a ton of metal, I'd have joined a gym."

Tyler pressed his face against the glass of a cage.

"Empty. How do we get in?"

"Through there." The boy indicated a side door. "It's one flight down."

"How do you ken that, titch?" Ryan asked.

"My class got a tour last month," Frankie replied. "We come here all the time."

He bit his lip.

"*Used* to come here all the time."

"You gonna lock yourselves in one of those cages?" Ryan looked doubtful. "It's a bit…" He searched for the right word. "Confining."

"Says the guy encased in armour," Oakley grunted.

"Ah prefer mobile defence suit." Ryan leaned back with a squeak.

"I dinnae want to go in a cage." Tyler eyed the glass box dubiously. "Reminds me of juvenile detention."

"What if a rhino or a hippo wanders in? Or anything else that ends in 'O'." Ryan struggled up and thumped the observation window with his sword. "This might be reinforced but they'll make short work of it."

"Rhinos and hippos can't handle stairs," Frankie pointed out. "And the top door is barricaded."

"Aw the same, me an Ty will take our chances ootside." He hoisted his sword. "Comin, big man?"

"Aye. This place pongs."

There was a thumping sound on the upper door and the boy halted.

"Or... maybe no. Cage suddenly sounds like a barry place tae be."

"That's not an animal." Oakley brushed past him. "It's someone knocking."

He pulled away the broom handle and unlocked the door. Brandon Golledge darted in, pushing his mountain bike.

"What happened to the others?" Oakley slammed the makeshift obstruction back in place.

"No time. Saw everyone come in here, so I thought I'd better warn you." The boy paused to catch his breath. "There's a lion right behind me and another two circling the building."

"Appreciate that." Ryan made for the staff room. "Let's get in that stinky room, pronto. Thanks for the heads up, blondie."

"Bad news is we've no idea when the next rescue will be," Brandon added. "Good news is, there's a rope ladder at the end of the zebra enclosure, if you fancy trying your luck."

"Not while there's lions on the prowl." Oakley shook his head. "You can hide in a cage with us till they go away."

"Got my own plans." The boy ran down the stairs and opened the doors, leaving them gaping. Then he sprinted back up and looked around.

"You have a death wish or something?" Frankie and Oakley were gawking at him.

"Get yourselves into one of those glass enclosures," Brandon urged. "I'll be fine."

"Fine? As in mauled to bits?"

"Trust me." He dragged the bench to the top of the stairs and tipped it over so the back hit the ground.

"*That's* no use as a barrier!"

"Not meant to keep anything out, don't worry."

"It's your funeral." Oakley dragged Frankie down to the next level and into one of the reinforced cages. Ryan and Tyler were already inside, hacking at an upright tree. It toppled over and crashed against the door, sealing it shut.

"Aw, that's nasty!" Tyler lifted one foot and scraped it on the glass, scoring a line down the surface. "I'm standin in monkey dood."

"Dirty wee bastards, eh?" Ryan began unfastening his armour. "What's that idiot up to?"

Brandon was sitting calmly on his bike, at the top of the stairs. There was a crash against the upper door and the broom handle shivered. Then another. But the reinforcements held.

"Any time now," the boy said to himself.

Two lions crept into the pavilion through the bottom entrance. Brandon gave a piercing whistle and pushed the bike backwards with his feet.

"That doughball is just *asking* tae get swallowed," Ryan spluttered.

With a deafening roar, the lions bounded up the stairs. Brandon stood on his pedals and shot forward to meet them.

His bike hit the back of the bench, as the creatures reached the top of the stairs. It whizzed up the home made ramp and shot into the air, sailing over the heads of the astonished predators.

Brandon cleared the steps entirely and landed on the tiled floor at the bottom with a sickening thump. The bike skidded across the polished surface and he slammed a hand into the wall to stop it toppling over.

Then he righted himself and rocketed out of the pavilion, pedalling furiously.

The lions gave a roar of fury and turned to chase him.

"In here kitty cats!" Tyler began pounding on the glass of the enclosure. "We're yer lunch, if you can get tae us!"

"Have you gone mental?" Ryan tried to pull him away. "Stop it!"

"That guy is too cool for school!" Tyler shoved the teenager back. "He's like Ghost Rider on a mountain bike. We got tae give him a chance."

The lions hesitated, unsure of who to go after.

"You are such a big softy." Ryan pulled off the last of his armour. Then he slid down his tracksuit bottoms and boxer shorts.

"Wee man?" Tyler covered his eyes. "That's makin me pretty uncomfortable."

"Check out *this* prime cut, Simba!" Ryan pressed his naked bum against the glass. "The butcher's department at Tesco doesnae have anything *near* as tasty."

Frankie giggled.

The lions bounded back up the stairs and sniffed around the cage, looking for a way in. Eventually, they realised there was no chance of reaching the occupants.

With a frustrated cacophony of snarls they turned and left again.

-22-

The Land Rover roared north east, past the dromedary and llama enclosures, heading for the top of the hill. Jamie was driving, with Siobhan in the passenger seat, recording the journey on her phone. Andrew and Man-Bok crouched in the trailer, holding onto the sides as it swayed from side to side.

"We'll be at the zebra paddock in five minutes at this rate," Jamie said triumphantly. "Once we get over the ladder, we can escape into the woods. Plenty of places to hide until we figure out what the hell is really going on."

He slammed on the brakes.

"Oh, no!"

A rhinoceros stood at the other end of the lane, pawing the ground, two clouds of breath erupting from flared nostrils.

"Reverse," Siobhan whispered.

"The path is too narrow to manoeuvre with the trailer attached." Jamie revved the engine. "Fortunately this vehicle weighs a couple of tons."

"How much does a *rhino* weigh?"

"About the same. But the Landover's made of metal."

"And that thing has a horn."

"So do we." The keeper slammed his hand on the steering wheel and a deafening drone filled the cab. "Maybe we can scare it."

The creature didn't move.

"In that case, I'll put a hole in it." Siobhan picked up the rifle. "Does it have any weak spots?"

"It's got more armour than a tank. Jump out and un-couple the trailer." Jamie fastened his seat belt. "I can't get up any kind of speed pulling it. It's the lever on the left."

"What are *you* going to do?"

"Ram the big sucker."

"Jamie!"

"If I don't incapacitate that thing, we're all toast. There's an injured kid back there. We can't even run."

Siobhan swung her mobile at him and pressed record.

"Say something."

"Ever the ace reporter, eh?" Jamie scratched his head awkwardly.

"Hi there, Kate. If I don't make it, I want you to know how much I love you and Gus. Gus? You're a fine young man and I know you'll grow up to be something special." He gave a grim smile. "Sorry, I don't have time to say more."

"Kate's your wife?"

"Ex-wife. Be quick."

Siobhan jumped out and unhitched the trailer.

"Leaving us behind?" Andrew's head popped up over the rim. "*That's* not cricket."

"Shut up." Siobhan slammed her hand on the side of the cab. "Done!"

The truck leapt forwards, rapidly gaining speed. Galvanised into action, the rhino charged to meet it, sandpaper hide scraping along the walls on either side of the path.

The two powerhouses collided with a deafening crunch. The bonnet of the Land Rover flew into the air as the front of the vehicle crumpled, gouts of steam billowed from the engine. The rhino's front legs buckled and went limp, its mighty head buried in furrowed metal.

The driver's door fell open and Jamie crawled out, blood running down his face.

"Thank God for air bags." He collapsed on the tarmac and gave them a weak thumbs up.

"You killed it!" Siobhan grinned. "You totally rock!"

"Thank you. But I'm going to have one hell of a headache." The man tried to stand. "Didn't really think I'd..."

The Land Rover exploded.

In an instant the vehicle, the rhino and Jamie were engulfed in a fireball, black clouds billowing into the air. The smell of burning petrol stung Siobhan's nostrils

"JAMIE!" She stumbled towards the inferno but was forced back by a shimmering curtain of heat.

"I HATE this place!"

Andrew helped Man-Bok out of the trailer.

"Brave guy," he muttered in shocked admiration.

The girl made one more attempt to reach the keeper, dancing round the edge of the flames.

"Siobhan!" Andrew grabbed her arm. "We need to get out of here before this draws even more attention."

"The bushes are catching fire," Man-Bok added. "And the wind is spreading the flames quickly."

"Just a minute." The teenager pulled out her mobile. "I have to record this."

"Jesus. Is getting a story so vital to you?"

"You're damned right it is!" Siobhan shook Andrew off. "Nobody's getting away with telling Jamie's son that he went crazy cause of a made up virus."

"Sorry." Andrew reddened. "I didn't mean any disrespect."

"I'll make sure he gets a *real* medal. Not some stupid award for rescuing a bloody cat out of a tree."

The pride of lions waited outside the ape house until they were sure the human occupants weren't coming out of their self-made prison. Then they loped north east until they reached the zebra paddock. They stopped and sniffed the air, hoping to catch the scent of other humans. But a stiff breeze was blowing westward, making it impossible.

Instead, the pride crept into the long grass close to the rope ladder, tawny coats providing the perfect camouflage among the dry stalks.

Then they settled down and waited for prey to arrive.

-23-

Yellow Leader strode into the control room and sat down. The radio operator handed him a headset and the soldier put it on.

Yellow Leader? A familiar voice crackled in his ear. *This is Brigadier General Moran. Have you assembled your team?*

"It was too short notice to get everyone, Sir."

You'll have to make do with replacements from the base. I want the ones most likely to follow orders without question. We've got two choppers ready to fly you to Edinburgh Zoo.

"What are my orders, Brigadier?"

Our cover story is that a deadly virus was released in the zoo. One that's affecting both animals and humans. We're saying it's a suspected terrorist attack. The police already sent in a squad, but they were massacred, so they've been told to create a perimeter and nobody is to get in or out.

143

"Massacred? So what exactly is going on?"

I wish I knew. Cloud cover and smoke are obscuring satellite pictures. You know as much as I do, Yellow Leader.

"You think anyone will actually fall for our excuse?"

I do. Cause here's the kicker. There really was a terrorist threat called in this morning.

"And you didn't engineer it?"

No. It came from an unidentified female inside the zoo. We've no idea who it was, but it's on the record and certainly backs up our story.

"Wow." Yellow Leader raised an eyebrow. "That's a stroke of luck."

I need experienced eyes on the ground to assess the situation. That's you.

"What are my orders? To locate TH4X 3?"

Negative. You won't have enough men or time.

"So, are we going in to rescue survivors?"

As far as we can tell, everyone in the zoo is dead. Which is a blessing in disguise. We can use the plague as an excuse to keep the place locked down until a larger squad can enter, eliminate the animals, and find TH4X 3.

"Then what exactly do you want my men to do? Stand around and look pretty?"

I understand your frustration, but this is a very shaky house of cards. The cover story will collapse if anyone gets out of that place and contradicts our version of events. Especially if they're given a clean bill of health.

"Sir? I don't understand."

Yes you do. I intend to delay a proper rescue for as long as I can. Let the creatures do our work for us. But there's always the possibility that someone in that place will be lucky enough to withstand their attacks.

"*That's* where we come in?"

You're there to make sure their luck runs out.

"With all due respect, Sir. We're talking about British citizens."

Your men have killed civilians before.

"Not our own."

Look. I seriously doubt it will come to that. From all reports, the zoo is a mass grave. You'll be issued hazmat suits, so make sure everyone sees you wearing them. That ought to drive home our point that a total quarantine is vital.

"Yes, Sir." Yellow Leader gripped the desk until his knuckles were pale pearls.

Retrieving TH4X 3 is a matter of utmost national security. We've already lost TH4X 1 and TH4X 2, so this is our last chance.

"Who came up with those stupid names anyway?"

Just do your job, Yellow Leader. I'm not asking you to call your kids after them.

"I'm extremely uncomfortable with this, Sir. For obvious reasons."

The wheels are set in motion, son. I can't do anything about that. It is what it is.

The Brigadier sighed loudly.

Over and out.

-Part 3-

A scientist based in Scotland claims to have found the first evidence of a common language shared by different animal species. The calls, which are understood by monkeys and birds, were discovered by Klaus Zuberbuhler, a psychologist at St Andrew's University.

According to Zuberbuhler, animals and birds can communicate complex ideas, not just to their peers, but across species.

The findings have been heralded as a significant breakthrough in the quest to discover the origins of human language and proof that the ability to construct a complex form of communication is not unique to man.

Sunday Times

-24-

"Looks like I'm your transport now." Andrew hoisted Man-Bok onto his back. "Glad you didn't have that sandwich, after all."

"Will you be all right carrying him?" Siobhan asked. "The fire from the Land Rover is beginning to spread and we'll have to go right round it to get to the ladder."

"You know what just occurred to me?" Andrew stayed where he was. "As soon as we headed for the zebra paddock, a sodding great rhino appeared in the way. Out of nowhere."

"Our luck hasn't been great. No denying it."

"I suspect it's more than that. Every time we make a move to escape, the perfect creatures to stop us seem to just… pop up."

He lowered his voice.

"It's like we're being watched."

"Even if the animals were smart enough to communicate with each other, how would they know exactly where we all are?" Siobhan looked up "I haven't spotted any birds in a while."

Andrew pointed to a security camera set on a pole.

"I'm talking about that."

"Someone's using CCTV to tell the animals where to cut us off?" Man-Bok broke in. "That's insane."

"And baboons ambushing a helicopter is a normal occurrence?"

"Smart is one thing," the Korean persisted. "Even I couldn't work a CCTV camera. I got problems operating a DVD player."

"They have *TV* in Korea?"

"Oh, you're a laugh a minute."

"Could be the missing keeper is alive, after all," Andrew mused. "If he was in the zoo all night, he might have mutated too. Maybe he's a sort of kindred spirit with the other animals and is organising this mayhem, somehow."

"After what we've experienced, I'm open to any dumb ideas." Siobhan unslung her rifle, took careful aim and fired. The camera jolted and a shower of sparks erupted from the casing.

"Consider the problem sorted."

"I don't think that will do much good. There are more dotted all over the zoo." Andrew thought hard. "Jamie mentioned a control centre next to the south wall. Must be that little red building we passed coming in this morning."

"I remember it." Siobhan checked her map. "It's not too far."

"What are you thinking?"

"I'll nip down there, fast as I can, and wreck the monitors. You take a detour round the fire then head for the ladder. I'll catch up."

"That's pretty risky." Andrew scratched his chin. "And how are you going to deal with whoever is watching us? Interview him to death?"

"Tell you what." Siobhan tapped her rifle.

"I'm actually looking forward to that part."

"You're actually pretty good in dangerous situations." Andrew nudged her. "You'll make a damned fine reporter."

Siobhan blushed.

Andrew and Man-Bok watched her sprint away.

"Which direction do *we* go?" the Korean asked.

"Anywhere a camera isn't pointing." Andrew set off. "Which is a shame, since I look pretty impressive carrying you to safety. It ought to be captured for posterity."

"Leave me behind, you big goon." Man-Bok pulled the boy's hair. "The bushes are going up like tinder and the wind is spreading the fire pretty fast. You can't outrun it lugging a dead weight."

"That's what mother and father would say." The teenager set off north at a brisk pace. "I already have enough baggage for their liking."

"Pushy parents?"

"They're determined I'm going to be a doctor when I graduate. Just like them. My own thoughts on the matter don't seem to count for much."

"It's a noble profession."

"Nobility doesn't come into it, MB," Andrew panted. "It's a way for me to make lots of money. Just like them."

He licked dry lips. "Well a doctor saves the injured, doesn't he?"

"Not by carrying them. You should have been a fireman."

"Actually, I quite fancy being a male model. I have excellent cheekbones." He showed the Korean his profile. "Feel free to agree."

"Are you *gay*?"

"Nope. Just extremely handsome." Andrew looked back. "Why? Are you?"

"Yes." The boy said quietly. "I've never admitted that to anyone before."

"I take it your aunt Chak wouldn't approve." Andrew stumbled and righted himself. "Especially since you have your legs round my waist."

"Don't worry. You're not my type."

"Then why tell me?"

"Might be the last chance I get to tell anyone." Man-Bok pointed to the flames vaulting from bush to bush.

"Andrew, the fire's too close and it's moving faster than us. We're not going to get round it."

Siobhan crouched behind a rose bush trying to decide on the best course of action. She wouldn't have bought Andrew's theory under any other circumstances. The idea that someone was watching them on CCTV and directing the animals was ludicrous. But so was everything that had happened today.

If it *was* true, she had a few small advantages. The control centre was in the southern part of the zoo and everyone else in her group was going north or west. That gave her the element of surprise.

She pulled out the little map on the zoo leaflet and studied it again. The control centre was fairly isolated, next to the Penguin Café and the gardener's huts, rather than any exhibits. It was unlikely that CCTV covered such an unimportant section. And it was downhill all the way.

Siobhan took a deep breath, then emerged from cover and began to run.

Her head swivelled from side to side, trying to look in all directions at once. Whenever she spotted a camera, she ducked out of sight until she could determine which direction it was pointing. Then she detoured around it and kept going.

A few minutes later, she was pressed against the pebbled wall of the control centre. She edged silently along the side of the building, ducking under the windows, until she reached the door.

The girl reached out slowly and inched down the handle, silently imploring it not to squeak.

It was locked.

Siobhan placed the barrel of the rifle against the lock and braced herself. She closed her eyes and pulled the trigger.

The rifle bucked violently in her hands and the metal shattered, slivers of steel rocketing past her head. Recovering, she kicked the door open and strode inside.

A large man lay dead on the floor, below a bank of monitors. The swivel chair next to him spun round.

Siobhan gasped.

In the seat was a chimpanzee, keeper's hat perched jauntily on its head.

The ape clutched the arms of the chair with leathery fingers. Its frightened eyes flicked right and left, looking for an escape route or weapon. On the table, just out of reach, was a tranc gun.

"Don't even think about it," Siobhan spat.

The chimp stared at her, sizing up the situation.

"I *mean* it."

The primate giggled, a noise so human that she flinched. Then it launched itself off the chair, arms outstretched.

Siobhan fired.

The bullet hit the ape in its chest and it landed in a writhing heap on the carpet. It turned and began crawling for the window, emitting plaintive wheezing noises. The girl sighted and pulled the trigger again.

The back of the beast's head imploded and it went limp, a puppet with cut strings.

There was no time to dwell on what she had just done. Siobhan dropped the rifle, sat down and studied the CCTV screens.

"Jeez. You were right, Andrew."

She could see all the areas of the zoo. On one screen was the burning Land Rover. Another showed the learning centre, Mondo peering nervously from one of the windows. Some displays looked down on scattered corpses. The monitors covering the zoo entrance revealed a multitude of animals hiding amongst the trees.

"So *that's* where you all are."

There was no sign of her other companions, dead or alive. She presumed that was a good thing.

The ape really *had* been monitoring them. And it was obviously communicating their whereabouts to the rest of the zoo's denizens. But how? It couldn't exactly phone them.

The hairs stood up on Siobhan's neck. She slowly turned and looked at the window.

Another chimp was watching her, rubbery face pressed balefully against the pane.

-25-

"Shit."

There was no way she could reach her gun and kill the creature before it raced off to warn the other animals. The chimp gave a victorious grin.

Something slammed into the ape from behind, squashing it against the glass. It gave an incredulous grunt and slid down the window, leaving a smear of blood on the pane.

Seconds later, Brandon Golledge appeared in the open doorway, holding a gardener's pitchfork.

"You born in a barn?" He closed the door behind him. "You'll let in more than a draught."

"Brandon!" The girl rushed over and hugged him. "How come you're always in the right place at the right time?"

"It's a Zen thing."

"The newspapers love a man of mystery. How about a short Q and A session?" Siobhan laughed nervously. "I'm kidding, of course. Sort of."

"Good, cause I can't really hang around." Brandon dropped the tool. "As if our immediate situation wasn't bad enough, the zoo now seems to be on fire."

"Our Land Rover exploded. Jamie's dead."

"Oh." Brandon nodded sadly. "Tough break."

"Why are you here, anyway?" Siobhan asked. "I thought you'd be well on your way by now."

"There!" Brandon indicated one of the screens. "*That's* what I'm looking for."

An abandoned skateboard was lying outside the camel paddock

"Why do you need a skateboard? You already have a bike."

"It's the owner I'm trying to find." Brandon tapped a monitor. "Hmmmm. Most of the animals are still gathered around the zoo entrance."

"I did notice."

"Damn. Right in the middle of my escape route."

"Brandon. Why don't they try to break out? They could make a fair go of it with only a cordon of police to stop them." Siobhan thumped the console in exasperation. "Even the birds are still perched in the trees."

"I think they're more interested in killing us than getting away," the boy shrugged. "Besides, where are they gonna go? They can't exactly take a bus into town."

"You'll never get past them. It would be suicide to try."

"Then they won't be expecting me. Gotta truck."

"Jesus, you got nerves of steel. That bravery award should be yours and you weren't even in the competition." Siobhan shook the boy's hand. "Good luck."

"You too." Brandon gave her a salute. "Keep on keepin on."

"Are you sure about this? Look. The rope ladder is still there." Siobhan pointed to a faint outline, almost invisible against the west wall. "We're all heading for it and there's safety in numbers."

"If you can see it, the ape probably could too," Brandon reminded her.

"You mean it might be a trap?"

"Does it matter? Whole zoo is a trap, far as I can see." The boy waved goodbye. "Push a chair under the door handle, if you're sticking around."

Then he was gone. Siobhan glimpsed him through the window, pedalling furiously uphill.

"I've got such a crush on that guy."

She raised her rifle to smash the screens then put it down again. The CCTV system must have been recording the zoo all night. Could there be a clue as to what had happened on the footage?

"I wonder."

She inspected the control panel until she found the rewind button. When she pressed it, the images on the screens began to jig backwards, growing dark as dawn retreated and night took over.

"There!" Siobhan paused the image and checked the time code at the bottom of one monitor. It read 3.10 am. She played the recording again and her eyes widened.

"What the hell am I looking at?"

A bright object suddenly streaked out of the night sky and landed in the zoo, lighting up the terrain with a fluorescent glow, before fading quickly away. It seemed to have come down near the ape enclosure.

"That's a missile of some sort!" She hunched forwards. "Is it a rocket? Why would anyone fire a rocket into the zoo in the middle of the night?"

She rewound the footage and played it one more time, recording the whole sequence on her phone.

"Maybe *this* is why the military quarantined the place." She tucked the mobile back into her pocket. "Somehow, they *caused* all the carnage. And I bet they don't want any witnesses to what they did getting free."

Siobhan broke the monitors with swift, decisive blows, in case any more primates decided to use it. She stood back and tapped her fingers together. They were shaking so badly she could hardly manage that simple action.

She grabbed the rifle and stepped out of the door.

The fire was being blown towards the control centre and it would burn down soon, taking all the evidence with it. But now she had the video clips on her phone.

Siobhan knew she already had the scoop of the century. One that would make her a celebrity. All she had to do was head for the ladder.

Only she couldn't. Real journalists didn't stop until they knew the whole truth.

Instead, she headed for the ape enclosure.

-26-

"No sign of Siobhan," Andrew wheezed, his pace markedly slower. "I hope she made it. I was… rather looking forward to being interviewed about my… exploits."

"If she did disable the cameras, she won't know where we are." Man-Bok sighed. "I'm too heavy for you, aren't I?"

"White man's burden, MB."

"The PC era just passed you by, huh?" the Korean snorted. "Put me down."

"I believe time is… of the essence."

"You can't outrun the fire carrying me." Man-Bok thumped the top of the boy's head. "See sense!"

"Don't muss my hair, MB."

"You are *impossible*!"

"I do… have to… rest for a minute." Andrew lowered his companion gently to the ground. "But animals are afraid of flames and the smoke is obscuring us. This is probably the best place we could be."

"And that's the dumbest thing I ever heard."

"Says the guy who broke his ankle falling off a dead giraffe."

161

"It feels a lot better now." Man-Bok poked his leg gingerly with one finger. "You go. I'll follow along at my own pace."

"Forget it." Andrew was bent over, hands on his knees. "All I need is… a little breather."

"Not if you're breathing in smoke." The Korean coughed. "You're totally exhausted."

"I'll get my second wind."

"The flames are closing in," Man-Bok pleaded. "*Please* leave me behind."

"That would seem the sensible option." The teen-ager made to pick up his companion again. "Good job I'm a prize idiot."

He stopped and straightened. "I heard something."

"One of the other kids, perhaps?" Man-Bok asked hopefully.

There was a crunching sound as if something large was barging through the greenery.

"Could be." Andrew drew the sword from his belt. "But it would have to be a very *fat* kid."

"It's coming this way." The Korean struggled upright, trying not to stand on his injured ankle. "And fast."

"You hobble off to that aquarium, there's a good fellow." Andrew indicated a low building just ahead. "I'll be there presently."

"Not without you."

"You'll just get in my way."

"What if it's that huge tiger?" the boy whispered. "Your sword won't do much good."

"Predators go after injured prey first, MB," Andrew hissed.

"I'll get moving." Man-Bok limped towards the Aquarium door, while his friend circled the bushes, weapon clutched in both hands.

"Come to daddy," he whispered. "Whatever you are, I'm going to put your ugly head on the wall of my bathroom."

A wild boar burst from the undergrowth, the hair on its back ablaze.

"Shit!" Andrew raised the sword above his head as the creature charged.

He brought the weapon down with all his considerable strength when the boar reached him. Its point entered the beast's neck, as 600 lbs of muscle slammed into his legs. A tusk sliced through flesh and Andrew let out a shriek of pain.

Boy and monster went down together.

Man-Bok came shambling back, wincing each time his foot touched the ground. Using the sword as leverage, he manoeuvred the tufted head off the teenager and slapped burning embers from his body.

"Sorry," Andrew whimpered. "I kind of stuffed that up."

Man-Bok pulled off his splint, wrapped the tie round Andrew's thigh and pulled it tight.

"Now, push with your good leg." He began to crawl, pulling his companion along.

"I can't," Andrew groaned. "It's too sore."

"Don't worry, you'll go into shock soon."

"Shock? I'm positively horrified." The teenager lay back, perspiration sheening his face. "I can't make it, I tell you."

"Come ON, you big pain in the butt." Man-Bok tugged harder. "Or I'll stick two fingers up your damned nose and drag you!"

"That would *not* be dignified, MB. Look, I'm shuffling along nicely."

Gasping and sobbing, they struggled into the aquarium, Man-Bok pulling the door closed behind them. Then he sank to the floor again, back pressed against the wood.

"You really can't walk?"

"Damned beastie's tusk tore through my tendons." Andrew examined the wound. "I'm grounded."

"You sure?"

"I was going to be a doctor, buddy." The teenager put a hand on his friend's arm. "You need to get out before this place burns down."

"It's made of concrete and full of water." Man-Bok nodded to brightly lit fish tanks lining the walls. "Got to be impervious to fire."

"But not smoke." Oily tendrils were wafting through the air vents. "Go and get my sword. Use it as a walking stick."

He groaned again. "You can't miss it. It's sticking out of a slab of crispy bacon."

"I can't. Not without my splint."

"Never rains but it pours, eh?" Andrew slumped against the boy. "Man-Bok, suddenly I don't... feel very well."

His jeans were soaked with blood and a dark pool was forming around him.

"Don't you fall asleep!" Man-Bok slapped his companion's face. "C'mon. What were you nominated for?"

"I wasn't." Andrew's eyes were glazed. "I stood in for one of my chums who was on manoeuvres with the T.A. Believe I mentioned it earlier."

He began to retch. Smoke was now pouring under the door, wreathing them in an acrid cloud.

"I was nominated cause I saved a cat stuck up a tree." Man-Bok pulled his jersey up over his nose and mouth. "Kind of ironic, eh?"

"I can't hear you. You're all muffled." Andrew's head lolled onto the Korean's shoulder. "I'm bushed, MB."

Man-Bok tested his foot by pushing it against the floor. A wave of agony swept up his leg. His eyes were watering so badly he could hardly keep them open and his head was throbbing.

"Hard to breathe," Andrew sighed. "So tired."

"Shhhh. You rest." Man-Bok put his arm around the boy. "Let's both have a little sleep, yeah? We'll make a run for it when we feel better."

"Mmmmm." The teenager's eyes slowly closed. "I'll get you back to aunt Chak. I promise."

"Course you will." Man-Bok kissed the boy on the forehead. "Your parents will be so proud of you."

"They will, won't they?" Andrew whispered, clutching his hand. "First time for everything."

His body went slack.

"I'm proud of you too." Man-Bok laid the boy on the cold stone floor.

Then he stretched out next to his friend and let himself drift into oblivion.

-27-

"Why we pushing through dese bushes?" Bangles grumbled. "It be takin for ever. We even goin in the right direction?"

"We're heading north to throw the animals off our track." Sammy ducked under an overhanging branch. "They're clever enough to know that any human trying to escape will usually take the shortest route and stick to the paths."

"They never set eyes on my cousin Top Top," the boy sniggered. "That peanut got hisself lost in Wal-Mart wid a frozen chicken down his pants."

"I won't even ask. Still, we're taking the long way and staying out of sight."

"Won't dey sniff us out?"

Sammy indicated the oily pall over the centre of the zoo.

"Not with that smoke in the air and dozens of corpses around. They're starting to smell a lot stronger than we do."

"Grody. But good news, I s'pose."

"You have a cousin called Top Top?"

"So? You got a boy's name."

"It's short for Samantha."

167

"Oh. Top Top's real handle be Demarion-Omar Crawford but dat sorry label is too much a mouthful for anyone. You *sure* you know where we going?"

"Uphill and away from that fire, till we reach the perimeter wall."

"We aint got the legs for that kinda jump, Sammy. Iss got more barbed wire on the top than World War One."

"I know. So we follow it east to the zebra paddock. The grass is long next to the barrier cause the zoo's mowers can't cut too close. We'll use it for cover."

"We aint gonna get too much cover from some overgrown lawn."

"We will if we crawl."

"Thass wack!" The boy pulled a twig from under his cap. "The animals be dead of old age by the time we get to the ladder, an I'll have worn holes in my knees."

"You rather the holes were made by something's teeth?"

"But we trying to get a swerve on! Thass a *long* ways."

"We'll crawl fast. Then we hide and wait for someone else to try for the ladder." Sammy pulled a clump of thorns aside to let the boy pass. "In case there are predators hidden somewhere, waiting for them."

"Reinforcements, huh? We all lock up and mob out together."

"No. We make a run for it while they're getting eaten."

Bangles checked to see if she was joking, but the girl's expression was steely.

"Thass pretty harsh, Sam."

"It's survival of the fittest."

"Well, you *are* seriously fit."

The girl glared at him.

"Don't be givin me the evil eye cause you punked by a compliment." Bangles held her stare. "You wanna act like some lone wolf gangster, thass your call. But it's beneath you, eh?"

He moved off.

"Sides, I seen plenty of *them* die."

Dax and Mondo sealed up every gap in the learning centre they could find. They had upturned tables against the doors and closed the wooden shutters on each window. Now they sat on the floor, waiting.

"We only have to hold on a little longer." Mondo twirled the scissors round his fingers. "Being in this place is safer than wandering around out there."

It was a sentiment he had repeated several times. Dax remained silent.

"My parents must be going crazy," Mondo continued. "Yours too."

"I wouldn't bet on it," Dax muttered darkly. "They kind of gave up on me a while ago."

"I shouldn't have made you stay." the boy said miserably.

"Nobody can *make* me do anything. That's my problem, apparently."

"Maybe we *should* try to run for it."

"It's too late." Dax opened the shutters a crack. "There's a grizzly bear out there."

"Oh, Christ." Mondo shuddered. "What's it doing?"

"Reading the *Sunday Times* and drinking sherry."

"Eh?"

"It's just sitting watching. Don't worry. It can't get past a barricaded door and the windows are too small for it to squeeze through."

"So I was right to stay here?"

"I wouldn't go that far." Dax plonked herself on the sofa and stared at the whiteboard on the wall. There were a few scribbled notes in red marker and the night shift workers' rota for the week.

"Mondo?" she frowned. "Check the keepers' timetable."

"What about it? It's just a bunch of people we don't know."

"Look at it properly, yeah?"

Mondo did. Then he paled.

"It says there were only four keepers staying here last night."

"Exactly. But Sammy said *five* beds had been used." Dax's eyes widened. "It's not a *keeper* that's missing. It's someone else."

She ran into the sleeping quarters, her companion right behind and threw back the covers on the empty mattress.

"I don't *believe* it."

"Now we know who was sleeping here." Mondo's eyes widened. "And who let the animals out."

"I have to warn the others."

"You'll die if you step out there," the boy wailed. "How are you going to get past the bear?"

"Got a rifle."

"Which would be dandy if you were a big game hunter." The boy glanced at the window. "Plus, there could be any number of beasts hidden round the corner."

"I'll have to take that chance." Dax put on her leather jacket.

Mondo quickly crossed the room and grabbed the gun.

"You'll get eaten." He pointed the weapon at her. "I can't let you go."

"What? You're going to *kill* me... to stop me being killed?"

"Point taken." Mondo slid the rifle behind the couch and pulled out his tranc pistol.

"A shot in the leg and you'll be out cold." The boy curled himself up on the sofa. "Sorry. We wait till the authorities arrive."

"I *stayed* with you," the girl glowered. "Even though I didn't want to."

"And you have no idea how grateful I am."

"So why are you acting like this?"

"Cause you're only one who did."

"And the others? What we've discovered could stop *them* getting killed."

"For all we know, they're already dead. You're alive and I intend to keep you that way."

"You little creep!" Dax exploded. "You'd leave everyone to their fate just to save your own skin?"

"Stop it. You're not thinking straight."

"Let me go, Mondo," the girl begged. "Or come with me. We can make it."

"We can't and you know it."

"Coward!"

"You can hate me. Call me names. It doesn't change anything." The boy stuck out his jaw. "I'm going to do *one* thing right. I *won't* let you die for nothing."

"That's not your decision to make, you bastard!"

"Sit down, Dax." Mondo motioned with the pistol, his voice laden with sorrow.

"I'm sorry but we're not going anywhere."

-28-

Brandon found his girlfriend's skateboard outside the camel enclosure at the top of the hill. It was pink, with a hand painted cherry on top. He stared at her mangled corpse a few feet away.

"Aw, Sandy." He kicked down the stand on his bike and dismounted. "Talk about wrong place, wrong time."

Averting his eyes, he propped the dead girl against a rock and went through the pockets of her torn jeans. Finally, he found a piece of paper.

"If I hadn't slept in, I'd be lying here with you."

He unfolded the bloody scrap and studied a diagram, scrawled in blue pen.

"Well set up. Wouldn't expect any less." He sighed. "We were going to pull off the most mental ride today. Over the roofs. Tops of fences. The works. Well, I still can. It'll just be more difficult with a pack of psychopathic animals trying to eat me."

He committed the information to memory and folded the paper again. Then he knelt down and clasped his hands together.

"Sandra White? You were the best skateboarder and free runner I ever met. A great kisser, too. I was completely in love with you."

Brandon pulled out his comb and fixed the girl's hair. Then he searched around until he found a bloody arm, studded with gravel. He reached into his rucksack and pulled out a ring.

"It's our six-month anniversary. I was going to give you this."

He pushed the ring onto one stiffened finger. It fitted perfectly. The body slid sideways and sprawled on the ground.

"Knew you'd see the funny side of it."

Gently putting down the arm, he began to cry. Hot salty tears streaked his grimy face and he buried his head in both hands. It took several minutes to finally get his emotions under control.

"I'm going to make a break for it now," he said. "I'll do you proud, I promise."

The body was looking at him with sightless eyes.

"Don't be like that, Sandy. You know what it will take to get out of here alive?" He ticked his fingers one by one. "Complete knowledge of the territory. The element of surprise. Most importantly, speed. I can't have anyone else slow me down."

He looked out across the zoo.

"The rest of these kids think I'm crazy but they're the ones who aren't going to make it. If I go back to help them, I'll be a goner too."

He picked up Sandy's skateboard and stuffed it into his satchel. Put her discarded baseball cap on his head, as a memento. In front of him, the path sloped steeply downwards. There was a lot of fire near the centre and it was spreading. He'd have to get around that while he still could.

Brandon pulled on his cycling gloves and looked at his own hands. They were sure and steady, as they always were before he did something insane.

"Bye girl." He blew her a kiss, eyes sparkling. "The world's going to be a lonely place without you."

Brandon rocketed downhill. He knew Sandy's carefully drawn up plans were useless, now that the animals had removed anything that could be used to scale the wall. He simply didn't have the heart to tell her, even if she was dead.

One last ride, then. He'd always been lucky, though it always seemed to be at other's expense. Perhaps he really would get out of this.

A lemur dropped from an overhanging tree and landed on his shoulders. Brandon sank his teeth into the creature's arm. The primate fell away, tumbling along the path in a jumble of spidery arms and bandy legs.

A dozen more attempted the same manoeuvre, but the boy zigzagged wildly – lashing out with his fists or shaking the beasts loose. Then the trees were gone and the tiny adversaries were left behind, screeching impotently. Brandon spun round a corner and whizzed straight through a pack of jackals, alerted by the lemurs' call.

The dumbfounded dogs skidded to a halt as the boy whizzed past. Then they turned and gave chase, emitting high pitched yelps.

"No going back now," Brandon panted.

He doubled his efforts, staying just ahead of the slavering pack. One jackal, swifter than the others, leapt at him. Brandon struck out with a booted foot and knocked it sideways. He stood up in his seat and pedalled harder.

He swerved through the gap in a nearby hedge and landed in the children's play park, jinking between swings, see-saws and bodies without slowing. The dogs were just as nimble, barely slowed by the obstacles.

Ahead was a huge mound of hardened sand that Sandy had marked on her map, probably for landscaping a new enclosure. Brandon shot up the man-made slope and hauled with all his might on the handlebars.

The bike sailed into the air and landed on the roof of the hippo enclosure. The jackals reached the apex of sand and stopped in dismay, unable to match his jump.

"Nice one, girl!" Brandon toppled off the bike and lay on his back, sucking in lungfuls of air. As his breathing returned to normal, he heard a faint *fhut fhut* above him.

He shielded his eyes with one hand. Half a dozen tiny objects sailed towards him.

"Helicopters!" he crowed. "Looks like the army have finally arrived."

But only two of the dots were choppers. The other four were growing in size too rapidly to be anything but birds.

The boy leapt on his bike. He turned away from the attackers and hunched his shoulders as if he were about to make a run for it. Instead, he suddenly flipped the bike up over his head and landed on his back again.

A snowy eagle crashed into the wheels and vanished over the side of the roof, trailing one broken wing. The other birds of prey pulled out of their dive, less than a metre above him. Brandon kicked with both feet, propelling the bike into the air. It clipped a falcon and the bird spun out of control and slammed into a nearby tree.

The boy caught the bike as it descended, jumped to his feet, then slammed the upside down aluminium frame into a skylight next to him. It broke straight through and Brandon followed it, landing on the concrete below in a shower of glass.

"Ooooh." He pulled himself into a ball. "That *hurt*."

The wooden door of the enclosure creaked open and a jackal bolted towards him, paws slipping on the wet surface. As it approached, the boy rolled over and plunged a huge shard of glass into the animal's neck.

The creature collapsed and thrashed around on the floor, coughing gouts of blood.

Struggling up, Brandon grabbed a fore and hind leg, swung the creature round twice and threw it as far as he could. The dog sailed through the air, then slid across the slimy stone, almost to the other side of the enclosure. Brandon could hear yipping sounds outside, as the other jackals realised this was the only place he could possibly be.

The dogs burst in, sniffing the air. Brandon's bike was propped beside the door, next to the keeper's mucking out equipment. At the other end of the long room, they saw their mortally wounded companion and scrabbled towards it.

Brandon threw the tarpaulin off the wheelbarrow he had been scrunched inside, grabbed the bike and pushed it into the light. He slammed the door shut and slid the bolt closed, as the jackals thudded against the other side.

Then he was off again, sticking close to the trees lining the path, in case those birds returned to the fray.

Private Mickey Guererro leaned out of his chopper.

"Down there!" he shouted. "There's a guy on a bike heading for the entrance."

Two more soldiers appeared over his shoulder.

"Is it a *kid*?" one asked. "He's going like a bomb."

"Not for long." Guererro took aim and let loose a torrent of automatic fire. Gouts of earth sprouted alongside the cyclist and he glanced up in astonishment.

"Missed him." The soldier let off another sustained burst, helmet jiggling around on his head. The boy weaved from side to side, trying to avoid the bullets.

A hand grabbed Guererro and pulled him back. It was his commander, Yellow Leader.

"What the hell are you doing?"

"Carrying out orders, Sir!" The private recited them insolently as if his commander had forgotten. "In the unlikely event of finding anyone alive, they are to be considered a threat to national security. Nobody is to get out."

Yellow Leader back-handed the man across the face. There was a stunned silence inside the copter.

"Wouldn't it be better for our cover story if it looked like animals killed them?" he snarled. "You idiot."

"With all due respect, *Sir*." The man resentfully touched the welt on his cheek. "He's heading right for the entrance."

"There are hundreds of bloodthirsty creatures and a wrecked vehicle under a tree in his way." The officer curled his lip. "Even if we were trying to *save* him he'd be screwed."

He rounded on the other soldiers.

"We're going into that hell, shortly," he commanded. "So forget the kid and start killing the bloody beasts."

Brandon's blood was boiling. The helicopter was *shooting* at him. Well, he was going to damned well make it, just to spite them.

He rounded another corner and slammed on the brakes. A vast herd of zebras, gazelles and wildebeest were charging up the hill towards him.

Brandon looked wildly around. No enclosures he could reach in time. No way he could retreat uphill faster than the beasts could run. He looked over his shoulder.

Another owl and a sea eagle were perched on top of a high fence, gazing unblinkingly at him.

"Sorry to disappoint you, guys." The boy clicked his finger at the birds. "But I go out my own way."

Then he cycled downhill towards the galloping herd.

-29-

"I smell smoke." Oakley sniffed the air. "That can't be good."

"Suit up, boy wonder." Ryan began to fasten on his breastplate. "It's high time we went fur a stroll tae that ladder."

"How are we gonna find it?" Tyler asked.

"Still got mah map, big man. zebra paddock's north east of here."

"Righto." Tyler put broad shoulders under the tree propped against the cage door and heaved. The trunk slid down the glass and crashed to the floor.

"I'm not sure armour will protect you if we run into lions," Oakley said doubtfully. "They're a lot bigger than wild dogs."

"He isnae wrong, wee man," Tyler agreed. "I'm a lover, no a fighter."

"That's what yir maw said to me the other night." Ryan sniggered. "Dinnae have a cow, though. The lions went after the tube on the bike."

"You don't know that," Oakley insisted. "And the weight will slow you down."

"What are *you* gonnae do? Outrun them? How fast do you think the kiddie can move?"

181

"Aye. Just stay at the back of us." Tyler stuck the helmet on his head. "Actually, that'd be quite good. I cannae see behind me, wearin this."

He tapped the metal visor.

"It should have wing mirrors, know?"

"I realise this is scary for you." Oakley knelt beside Frankie. "Quite frankly, I'm bricking it, myself."

"Why don't we stay here?"

"Cause there's no smoke without fire, kid."

"There are hoses for cleaning out the cages. We could use them."

"I dinnae want tae rust," Tyler broke in.

"We'd have to come out of the cage to use hoses," the teenager explained patiently. "Then we'd be sitting ducks."

The little boy nodded.

"So we'll stay behind the two chavs. Let them do the fighting."

"Less of the chav, pal." Ryan pulled himself up to his full height of five feet three. "The proper term is *neds*."

"Non Educated Delinquents," Tyler added proudly by way of explanation.

"You dinnae find chavs wearin fine trackie suits like ours."

"Aw mornin fightin nature and I'm still gleamin white." Tyler inspected his outfit. "Damn. I got a smudge on mah top."

"You two are something else."

"We'll take that as a compliment." The teenagers continued to don their armour.

"If we get attacked, I want you to run and hide, fast as you can." Oakley gripped the child's shoulders. "Understand?"

"What about you?"

"Don't worry." Oakley indicated Ryan and Tyler, looking like slightly tarnished Arthurian knights. "I've got two of Edinburgh's finest hard men protecting me."

"We'll keep you and your mate safe," Tyler patted Frankie's head with an iron glove.

"Ouch."

"Sorry." He backed away. "I'm just trying tae say, I'm no gonnae let any wee lad get eaten. Unless it's Ryan."

"I'm too stringy, chunky boy. They'll head straight for a meaty lunk like you."

Frankie bit his lip.

"Thanks," he said quietly. "But I really think we should stay here."

"Why is that?"

The child cupped his ear

"Because I can hear shooting."

Brandon was twenty feet from the herd. Close enough to see their rolling eyes and steaming breath, as they galloped towards him.

"Move along now." He rang the bell on his handlebars and it gave a pathetic *ting*. "I got right of way!"

He winced. Not exactly memorable as last words.

The choppers opened fire again and the front row of the massed herbivores exploded in a mass of blood and gristle, torn apart by the mounted cannon.

The boy threw himself off the bike and covered his head, as the animals were torn apart. Trees and bushes shuddered, sending up fountains of leaves and the remaining beasts scattered in all directions.

"Bruce Willis eat your heart out!" Mickey Guererro whooped, hanging out of the helicopter and pouring volleys down into the creatures. "They're bound to make *this* into a movie!"

A sea eagle materialised in the open doorway and crashed into him, sinking massive talons into the man's chest. It gave a powerful beat of its wings and pulled Guerrero out of the copter. With a scream, he plunged towards the ground, locked in a deathly embrace with the bird.

The owl followed its larger companion, straight into the helicopter. It pecked and bit until the soldiers overpowered it, clubbing the creature with the butts of their rifles.

"Jesus, these monstrosities really mean business." Yellow Leader kicked the owl's corpse out of the open doorway.

"Land in the car park outside the gate, right now, before one of them decides to fly into the rotors."

Brandon heard a thump as the gunfire faded away. Mickey Guererro was crumpled on the path, a pool of blood spreading from his broken body, mingling with the feathers of the dead eagle.

"Should have watched the birdie," the teenager spat.

A carpet of animal carcasses, stretched right to the bottom of the hill, some still twitching.

"I'm not dead." The boy got on his bike, shaking his head in disbelief. He cycled carefully between the corpses, tyres squelching through red goo.

"I'm not *dead*!"

There was a growl behind him and Brandon slowly looked back.

A gigantic Bengal tiger crouched on top of a dead wildebeest, glaring at the boy. It opened its mouth revealing rows of yellow teeth.

"I'm dead."

He pumped the pedals, wasting valuable seconds, as the wheels spun in gore. Then he cleared the carnage and began to gather speed. The tiger leapt from carcass to carcass in powerful bounds, quickly gaining on him. Brandon looked for any avenue of escape.

"Don't stop shooting!" he implored, glancing up at the helicopters. But the guns had fallen silent, as the choppers approached the wall of the zoo.

Then he had an idea.

Brandon veered right, away from the main gate and towards the penguin enclosure. The observation window had been shot to pieces and all the water was gone. With a well-practised jump, the boy cleared the jagged shards and cycled into the empty pool, Sheridan only yards behind.

Above him, the second chopper filled the sky, its undercarriage already lowering in preparation for landing.

Brandon's knees felt like they were about to pop out of their sockets. He had to summon one last ounce of strength. The boy stood up and pedalled like he had never done before. He reached the curve of the penguin pool and soared up the incline, past the lip and into the air.

The boy felt a blast of hot air on his back and the tiger's jaws clamped on the wheel of the cycle.

Brandon opened his legs and let his trusty steed fall away, reaching up with both hands.

-30-

Bangles and Sammy crawled through the long grass, shoulders almost touching the wall.

"I juss put my hand in something nasty and little flies be whizzing up my nose," Bangles complained. "For the first time, I'm thinking there *are* fates worse than death."

"Couldn't agree more," Sammy snapped. "I've been listening to you complain for ten solid minutes."

"You just agitated cause you're scared, betty. No need to be a hater."

"That obvious, eh?"

"For shizzle. And I aint complaining, juss shootin the breeze. But iss hard to think of something light-hearted."

"Please try. I'm finding it difficult to hold things to-gether."

"Then be easy for a while." Bangles stopped in a small thicket of trees by the wall and propped himself against a trunk. "We well hid here."

"You were the one who insisted on hurrying!" Sammy gawped. "Look at all the smoke below us now. We can't hang around."

187

"Iss all good." The boy held up a finger. "Wind be blowing the flames west and we heading east. We gots time."

"What? You're Bear Grillis all of a sudden?"

"Who dat?"

"Never mind." Sammy kept crawling. "Wind can change direction, you prat."

"Hey! Let's chop it up, bossy." The boy grabbed her belt and yanked Sammy towards him. As she scrabbled to get free, he pulled a flick knife from his pocket.

"Don't hurt me." The girl looked cowed. "I didn't mean to insult you."

"Quit being a fizzle," Bangles snorted.. "*Chop it up* means have a conversation."

"Oh."

"Your hands are bleedin an I know they must be paining you." Bangles sliced the lower half of his T-shirt away and began to wrap it round the cuts. "They soft as butter."

"Thank you."

"Now take a break, feel me? Or you won't be able to climb that ladder. You shakin like a tweaker who lost her welfare cheque."

"I suppose we could rest for five minutes."

"Make it two. I aint *that* much of a… prat. I'm assuming that's a diss, huh?"

"Yeah. Sorry."

They sat and looked out over the vista. The north wall crested the hill and they could see across the whole zoo, with a housing estate beyond and Edinburgh laid out behind it, all the way to the Pentland Hills.

"Nice view. Almost as pretty as Chicago."

"Look," Sammy gasped. "Helicopters!"

Two choppers were heading towards the zoo entrance.

"Looks like the cavalry finally arrived."

"I'd be jumpin with joy if dey weren't landin a mile away." Bangles grabbed her arm. "Hey! Aint that Brandon? Can't be anyone else on a bike in dis place."

An ant sized figure was cycling furiously down one of the paths. Sammy's face dropped, as tiny sparks erupted from the helicopter door.

"Bangles. They're *shooting* at him."

"Then they aint no hazmat team," the boy cursed. "An dose mothers sure as shit aint here to rescue anyone. They trying to *stop* Brandon getting out."

"But… but *why*? We don't *have* any plague. Don't they realise that by now?"

"I reckon they do, but we can suss it out later." The boy squeezed her hand. "Let's juss stay hid until they landed. Then we keep movin to dat ladder."

"I'm really scared," Sammy whispered. "I don't understand what's going on."

They sat back to back, staring up through the leafy braches, trying to comprehend what they had seen. Sammy was shaking, clenching and unclenching her fists.

"You ever hear of a moon tree?" Bangles asked.

"Is this a *quiz*?"

"Hey. I be makin light-hearted conversation, like you axed."

"Ok. I'll bite." The girl tried to calm her ragged breathing. "What's a moon tree?"

"Back in 1971, Apollo 14 orbited the moon. One of dem asternoughts used to be a forest firefighter, so he took a bunch of tree seeds with him. They all got planted in different places when he brung them back. Then everyone forgot about them. I'm keepin this 100%."

Bangles looked mystified.

"How could you forget about trees dat had been to the *moon*?"

"Never heard of them," Sammy admitted, scratching her bandaged hands.

"My daddy told me one got planted in his hood," the boy continued. "Said it was part of some half assed scheme to improve the projects. Nobody else knew bout it, on account the plaque telling the story got jacked right away. But he remembered, cause he was the one what stole it."

Bangles smiled.

"He tole me that even a seed growing in the ghetto could be special."

"Sounds like a wise man."

"Naw. He was a thirsty towel. Cut off bits of the tree to sell as souvenirs, so the damn thing died."

Bangles took off his cap and studied it.

"Daddy got arrested for vandalism and fraud. The laws thought he be makin the whole shebang up. Don't know I fell for his weak sauce story myself."

"This is light-hearted conversation?"

"Iss an analogy, breezy."

"You finally said a word I understand."

Bangles looked hurt.

"That was uncalled for." Sammy glanced at him shyly. "Please go on."

"The place I come from cuts bits of you away until you wither an die, no matter how special you wanna be. Thass what I'm trying to convey."

Bangles folded his arms.

"But I aint going down that road, an I refuse to be forgotten. I aint no brainbox, but I stuck at school an got on a music exchange programme here. I write my own tunes. I study. I go hard."

He gave her a wan smile.

"Gonna reach for the stars, even if dey too far away to grasp."

"That's very poetic. Shame you ended up here."

"For sure. This turf be even worse than where I was raised. But that didn't beat me and neither will the zoo. Or those bozos in the chopper."

He turned to her.

"You a straight-A student, I'm guessing."

"I am."

"Then you already a lot closer to your goal than I'll ever be," the boy said pointedly. "But it won't mean squat if you aint gots no self-respect."

"Don't lecture me. Right now I'm more concerned with surviving than feeling good about myself."

"What I'm sayin is, you aint no hard ass. You a good person." He patted her leg. "So, we see any others in trouble, we gonna help, feel?"

Sammy went red.

"I just don't want to die, Bangles. I'm fifteen, for God's sake."

"I hear dat. Kinda fond of living myself." He winked at her. "More so, now I gots you to hang wid."

"You're funny and brave and smart." Sammy bit her lip. "I don't know *why* you've stuck with me."

"Ditto. Most bougie crackers here wouldn't give me the time of day."

"Bougie crackers?"

"Middle-class white folks, I guess you'd say. Think I gonna car-jack em or somethin."

"I'd probably have been the same," the girl admitted, going even redder. "In other circumstances."

"Then this aint so bad a place," Bangles laughed. "Iss bringing out the best in us. In other *circumstances* I might juss be stealin you purse."

"No you wouldn't. You may be tough but you're definitely one of the good guys. You make me feel ashamed."

"Don't swell my head, betty." He took the girl's hands and studied them. "Not great, but they'll have to do. You ready to dip out?"

"Not yet." Sammy held on. "You still want to go for… what was it? Bites? When this is over?"

"You know it. An I aint talking MacDonald's. You got class an I wanna show respect, but I aint too articulate. Don't have much cash, neither."

He shrugged.

"I could always hold up a gas station."

"Petrol station."

"Like I say, I aint very articulate."

"Really? Then why is that the most romantic thing anyone ever said to me?"

"Cause you gots low eggspectations?"

"Not anymore." Sammy leaned over and kissed the boy on the lips. She leaned back and put a hand to her mouth.

"I've never done anything like that before!"

"We be having a few new experiences today, thass for sure. You the first white boo I ever locked lips with."

"Boo?"

"Eh… It's a girlfriend." The boy rubbed his eyelid. "I know that won't mean nothin when we get outta here…"

"Don't be too sure, Bangles. Suddenly I've got a lot of living to do."

"I hear that! We set?"

"Yeah. But you go first so I can check out your ba-dink-a-dink," the girl smiled. "Boo."

"Woah! You hella bold, all of a sudden."

"My whole life I've been blending into the background." Sammy kissed him again. "Took something like this to realise how much I hate it."

-31-

The choppers landed in the car park and soldiers wearing hazmat suits poured from the interior. Yellow Leader strode over to the Police Chief.

"Sorry about your Armed Response team," he said brusquely. "We'll be taking their armoured vehicle into the zoo and skirting the fire to search for survivors. Tell your men to concentrate on patrolling the perimeter." He looked around.

"Where *are* your men?"

"A lot of them took off when they saw you coming." the chief was sweating under his gauze mask. "What did you expect? They're terrified of catching this plague."

He pointed downhill to a cluster of boxy dwellings.

"We've already emptied the housing estate but the roads leading away are clogged up. Why are no phones working? People can't even call 999."

"It's a new protocol, under anti-terrorist laws. The exchange has been told to jam all signals. You can use a phone to set off a bomb, you know."

"If you're being so damned careful, why didn't you quarantine the boy?" The chief couldn't hide his frustration. "We were told there were no survivors. Suppose he's infected?"

"Eh? *What* boy?"

"The one who was clinging to the wheels of your chopper, of course." The policemen looked around, frowning. "Wait. Where's he gone?"

A tiny figure on a skateboard was vanishing down the hill towards the housing estate. Brandon raised a middle finger to them as he disappeared.

Yellow Leader's jaw dropped.

"Anderson. Wooten," he yelled. "Take four men each and stop him! Use any means necessary." He rounded on the chief.

"Keep this incident under your hat until we get the kid," he threatened. "Or you'll be up on charges of treason."

"He's wearing a baseball cap, like 99% of teenagers these days." The chief stuck out his chin. "If he mixes with the evacuees, you'll never pick him out. You don't even know what he looks like."

"He won't be leaving the housing estate," Yellow Leader growled. "I guarantee it."

Hidden in a tree, a large black ape watched the proceedings intently. Behind him, smoke was rolling over the terrain, as the fire crept inexorably towards the entrance. It gave a resigned grunt, raised one muscular arm and waved it in the air. Then it bounded east, using massive knuckles to propel itself.

The other animals, hidden round the entrance, slowly turned and began making their way back into the zoo.

Siobhan waved frantically as the army helicopters passed overhead but there were too many trees and bushes for them to spot her. Maybe it was for the best. After witnessing the footage in the control centre, she wasn't sure if she trusted the occupants.

Instead, she jogged towards the ape house, ignoring any cover. The cameras were useless now and she knew most of the animals were clustered round the entrance.

She wondered where Andrew and Man-Bok were, but couldn't take the time to detour. She glanced uphill, towards the pall of smoke, shrouding burning treetops. The night keeper's quarters were up there and she hoped Dax and Mondo had the sense to get out before they were surrounded by flames.

When she looked back at the path, two chimpanzees stood in her way.

"Oh God."

One primate bared its teeth and pointed at her. The other jumped around behind its companion, gibbering excitedly. Siobhan slowly unslung her rifle, trying not to make any sudden moves.

"This is a boom stick," she rasped. "Get lost or it'll kill you. I'm a good shot too."

The apes moved a few feet back, screeching in fury, but refused to retreat. They smacked wrinkled hands on their chests, making little runs towards the girl. Siobhan frowned.

"I thought you were supposed to be brainy." She lifted the gun to her shoulder. "Working together with your little furry friends, not standing there like a couple of carnival ducks."

The words caught in her throat.

Working together.

She whirled round. A leopard was streaking towards her, a smear of yellow and black.

Siobhan fired instinctively.

It was a lucky shot. The bullet hit the creature between the eyes and it died mid-pounce. The cat slammed into her, knocking the rifle from the girl's hands.

The chimps stopped keening and advanced, suddenly calm and purposeful. No more chattering or jumping. One gave a triumphant grin.

Siobhan pulled the tranc gun from her belt and levelled it at them. The apes looked at each other, then turned and fled into the undergrowth.

"Not *too* clever then." The girl wriggled out from under the dead cat. "I haven't got any darts left."

She finally freed herself and retrieved the rifle.

There was a rustling sound to her left, coming from a thicket of trees. She pulled the trigger in panic. The shot whistled harmlessly through the leaves. There was a whoop from the right and she turned and let off another round.

Nothing.

Siobhan suddenly realised what the chimps were up to.

"You're trying to make me use up my ammo," she hissed. "Sneaky little…"

The girl tried to stay composed, but the image of a dozen apes tearing her limb from limb leapt, unbidden, into her head. With a cry, she began to run, swinging the weapon from side to side. More bushes rustled as the pursuers kept pace, just out of sight.

A stone hit her in the back of the head and she sprawled across the asphalt.

The apes sensed victory. Leaves parted on all sides and Siobhan found herself surrounded by a ring of snarling chimpanzees.

She didn't have enough bullets to bring them all down. The creatures gestured to each other, screeching and smacking their lips, plucking up the courage to make a unified rush.

"Sod off, you hairy bastards. I'm not dying *that* way." With a sob, Siobhan sat up, put the barrel of the gun under her chin and reached for the trigger.

A huge primate, black as night and just as menacing, swung down from a tree and landed in front of her. With a dismissive swipe, it knocked the rifle from her grasp.

Siobhan pulled out her mobile and began to film the attacker. Maybe nobody took her seriously but she *was* a reporter and she'd damned well go out like one.

"Kill me in cold blood then," she stammered with false bravado. "Show the world you're no better than us."

Holding the mobile like a shield, she closed her eyes tightly, waiting for the blow that would end her life. It didn't come.

She opened them again

The black ape sat on its haunches, staring intently at her as if it understood what she had said. Suddenly it stood up and bared yellow teeth at its companions. Another beast, almost as large, rose to challenge the leader. The chimp let out a protective roar and shuffled towards the upstart, beating its shiny chest. The underling dropped back down and retreated, followed by the rest of the troop.

The ape picked up the rifle and regarded it with distaste. Then it handed the weapon back.

"Thank you," the girl whispered. "Nobody likes bad press, I guess."

The creature gave a disgusted snort and loped away.

The mysterious escape had galvanised her and she struggled to her feet. Shouldering her rifle, Siobhan began walking, her legs growing steadier with each step.

-32-

Mondo peered out of the window for the fourth time in as many minutes.

"Smoke's getting thicker." Dax was seated on the floor at the other end of the room, scowling at him. "What are you looking at?"

"The trees around the learning centre are on fire." A bead of perspiration trickled down the boy's face.

"Any chance of me taking a peek?" Dax studied black painted fingernails. "Or do you think I'll dive head first through the glass?"

"Not anymore." Mondo waved her over. Dax got up and opened the shutters.

The trees around Wilson Park were shafts of sparkling orange, and smoke billowed from the door of the Reptile House.

"If we don't leave now, this building will go up next," she said listlessly. "This part of your plan for saving me?"

"The Reptile House is at least thirty feet away." The boy gripped the sill until his knuckles were white. "And there's a big stretch of grass and gravel between us and the trees."

"Grass burns, you tool. The wind's blowing the fire right towards this building."

"I know." Mondo stuck his hands in his pockets, refusing to look at her. "I was just trying to keep you safe."

"So you keep saying." Dax looked out again. "I don't see any animals. Maybe cause they're smarter than us and don't intend to be incinerated."

"Get your rifle." The boy slumped down on a chair. "Make a run for it. I'll cover you with the tranc guns I have left."

Dax didn't need a second invitation. She retrieved her weapon from behind the couch and made for the door. Mondo lined up his darts along the coffee table.

"I screw everything up, you know," the boy said morosely. "This was just bigger than most."

Dax hesitated.

"C'mon. We'll go together."

"I told you. I'm not leaving."

"This place *will* burn down. And soon." Dax strode over and kicked Mondo in the shin. "You really think the flesh melting off your bones is worse than getting eaten?"

"Will you shoot me if something starts tearing me apart?"

"No. I'd be wasting a precious bullet."

"That's honest." Mondo began to sob.

"I'd shoot the animal though." Dax crouched down next to him. "I promised to keep you safe, remember?

I keep my promises, even when the other person turns out to be a total pain."

She reached out her hand.

"Collect your darts and let's get moving."

"Wait." Mondo wiped his nose with one grubby sleeve. He picked up a cleaning bucket and filled it with water from the sink.

"What are you doing? We don't have time for…"

Mondo emptied the bucket over Dax's head.

"You little…!" the girl spluttered, wiping sodden locks from her forehead. "It took me two hours to spike up my hair."

"It'll protect you from the flames." Mondo filled the bucket again. "Mask your scent as well."

"Oh." Dax shivered. "Very clever."

The boy poured the second bucket over his own head.

"Oooh. That's cold!" he shuddered, spraying drop-lets everywhere. "Maybe the shock will bring me to my senses."

"About time." His companion unlocked the door and yanked it open. "Elvis has left the building!"

They raced into a blast of heat, then skidded to a halt.

The grizzly bear was waiting for them.

Oakley, Ryan and Tyler crouched near the upper door of the ape house. Frankie stood nervously behind them.

"I don't want to leave," he repeated. "I'm afraid."

"When I was a kid, there used tae be a gang in mah street that took the piss oot of me," Ryan said. "I was too scared to go oot an play in case they gave me a kickin."

"This is a good story." Tyler grinned.

"I'll never forget the advice mah faither gave me."

"What was that?" Frankie asked.

"He said if I didnae leave the hoose and stop hassling him, he'd beat the shit oot of me hisself." Ryan smiled at the memory. "Had a way with words, did dad."

Oakley groaned.

"So you fought the gang?" The little boy's eyes were wide.

"Nah. I made friends wi Tyler and he battered them. Nobody messes with that big raj. He's got a temper."

"There's no much I *am* good at," his companion said proudly. "But I know how tae use mah fists."

He knelt by the child, metal hinges at his knees creaking loudly.

"I'm like Iron Man wi this armour on," he whispered. "Same as in the comic books, eh? You like comic books, Frankie? Ahm no much of a reader but I'm a big fan o the Hulk, cause I lose my rag a lot, like Ryan says. An I love Wolverine cause o the claws that come oot his wrists. No so much when he wears that twatty yellow number, mind, but his leather jacket is totally cool. I've got wan just the same at hame."

"I used to like Spiderman," the child ventured.

"Ach, I cannae be doin with poncy superheroes that wear tights." Tyler snorted. "What's aw that aboot? Crime fighters shouldnae look like ballet danglers. They'd be as well scrappin in their jammies."

"You better change the subject, wee man." Ryan winked at Frankie. "Get him talking aboot comics and we'll be here aw day."

"This is mah chance tae be a real superhero, y'know?" Tyler nudged the boy, almost knocking him over. "Guys like me dinnae get that opportunity very often."

He pushed down his visor.

"But you need tae gie me a cool name, so I can act the part right."

"What about Captain Clanky?" Oakley suggested.

"Dumbzilla?" Ryan added.

"Mind what I said about mah temper?"

"I'll shut up, big man."

Frankie thought hard.

"The Crusher?"

"The Crusher? That's epic!" Tyler grinned. "Ryan can be mah sidekick, the Wee Pounder."

"The *Wee Pounder*? Makes me sound like a bargain store."

"The Crusher and the Wee Pounder are gonna get you oot of this zoo, Frankie." Tyler stood up. "Or die trying."

"Hold off with the death bit, you big munter."

"Call me Crusher."

"Aye. Whatever."

"You want to ride on my shoulders, Frankie?"

"I'll look after him." Oakley quickly took the boy's hand. "I got him separated from everyone else. He's my responsibility."

"Oakley's right." Ryan agreed. "You swing that sword around when he's up there and you'll slice the kiddie's nose aff."

"That's why you're the smarts o this crime fighting duo, Wee Pounder."

"One." Ryan ticked his gauntleted fingers. "We're no fightin crime. We're fightin animals. Two. We've never been on the right side of the law in oor lives. Three. Call me Wee Pounder again an I'll stick a pound of fist right through that visor."

"Can we *go* now," Oakley pleaded.

"Don't leave without saying goodbye. I just got here."

The group whirled round.

Siobhan Mills stood at the bottom of the stairs.

-33-

"Siobhan!" Frankie ran down and hugged the girl. "Where have you been?"

"I stopped for ice cream cones." The girl squeezed him back. "Pity they melted on the way. A lot of the zoo is on fire."

"I've had five already." Tyler flipped up his visor. "Hello gorgeous. You've... eh... got a bit of blood on you."

"Vendor tried to overcharge me." Siobhan looked at the suits of armour, bemused. Then she quickly recovered. Nothing was unexpected any more.

"Nice outfits, guys. Glad to see you're fine Oakley. I'll get that interview at a more appropriate time."

"*Fine* isn't exactly the word I'd use." The teenager beamed at her. "But I'm all the better for seeing you. This is Ryan and Tyler."

"Call me The Crusher, doll. And this is..."

"Dinnae even go there, big man." Ryan glowered. "Pleased to meet you, toots. Spot any beasties in the vicinity?"

"Apes." Siobhan let go of Frankie and marched up the stairs. "And here's the crazy part. They had me at their mercy, not five minutes ago, but their leader let me walk away. Not that I was walking, mind you."

"Where are they now?"

"No idea. But it can't be far."

"We need to head for the ladder before they arrive." Oakley peered out of the door again. "Looks like the coast is clear."

"Wait!" Siobhan held up a hand. "You see anything unusual in the ape house?"

"Apart from some lions, a lunatic on a bike and two knights of the round table?"

"Something like a rocket. Or a missile."

"Eh... No."

"Us neither." Ryan looked around. "What aboot you, Frankie?"

His brow furrowed. "Frankie?"

"How did he vanish so fast?" Tyler gaped. "That kid would be sorted as a shoplifter."

"Check the cages!" Oakley pushed past Siobhan. "I'll look out the bottom door."

Half way down the stairs the teenager stopped. He hadn't noticed before but each ape house occupant had a framed photograph, mounted on the wall, with their names recorded on rectangular plaques.

Ewan. Maisie. Gordon.

Suddenly he remembered what Frankie had said back in the learning centre.

Satan is in control of this place.

A picture of a huge chimp took pride of place in the primate gallery. It was jet black and the craggy features looked inscrutably out of the frame, like some hairy Mona Lisa.

Oakley blanched.

Underneath was the ape's name.

Satan.

Dax and Mondo fled back to the keepers' quarters, the bear close behind. The girl tried to slam the door shut, but their ursine pursuer was too fast. Slamming both paws on the wood, it forced the door open, throwing Dax into the air. She landed on the coffee table, breaking it in two.

The bear began to wriggle into the narrow entrance. Mondo grabbed the rifle and cocked it. The bear surged forwards and the frame buckled as the beast tried to pull its hindquarters through the gap. It punched at Mondo with giant paws, spraying back globules across the wall, its face expressionless.

Mondo remembered reading that bears were the only predators who showed no expression when they attacked.

He fired at point blank range.

This time, the bear looked positively astonished. Its eyes crossed and it sagged, lifeless, in the doorway. He lifted the gun again.

"Don't waste bullets," Dax warned. "You killed it."

"Let's go out the window." Mondo pulled open the shutters. "Oh… my… God."

The keeper's quarters were ringed by a vast array of creatures, all staring at him. Behind them, the reptile house was a sea of flames, turning the sky orange and casting the creature's flickering shadows into hulking, misshapen forms.

"So *this* is what hell is like," Dax grimaced.

But Mondo was looking at the ground outside. He silently closed the shutters, barred them, and ran over to the bear. He gingerly lifted a paw and sniffed it.

"Get into the bedroom," he commanded. "We don't have much time."

"I know teenage boys think about sex every eleven seconds, but I'm really not in the mood."

"Pull the mattresses off the beds and cover yourself with them. Now!"

"That's not going to fool the beasts."

"The bear's paws are covered in petrol." Mondo pointed to the black stains on the wall. "It must be leaking out of the chopper. And the fire is reaching it."

He dragged the girl into the bedroom and they began hauling mattresses off the beds. In the next room, they could hear shutters splintering as smaller creatures forced their way in.

"Lie here." Mondo pushed Dax down and began piling the mattresses over her.

"What are you doing?"

"I'll hold them off."

"You will not!" The girl grabbed his arm, trying to squirm out from the downy shield. "It's my rifle."

Mondo slammed his elbow into her forehead. Dax sank back with a yelp. The boy climbed on top of the pile to stop her getting up again.

The door burst open and a fox bounded through. Mondo fired and the animal somersaulted back into the main room.

"One down!" the boy shouted. "Who's next!"

The doorway remained empty.

"What are you waiting for? Christmas?" Mondo's nerves were stretched to breaking point. "Come *on*, damn you!"

Silence.

"Too scared, eh?"

Then they erupted through the door. Gophers, otters, tamarinds, lemurs. Small furry mammals the boy couldn't even identify. With a howl of rage, he reversed the rifle and began to swing at them.

The miniature adversaries swarmed up his legs, biting and clawing. Within seconds, he was covered, fighting desperately to keep them away from his face.

As he fell backwards, disappearing behind the pile of mattresses, a chunk of the burning reptile house peeled away from the main building and landed on the petrol soaked ground outside.

A dazzling white light filled the bedroom and a giant fireball ripped through the keeper's quarters.

-34-

"Frankie!" Oakley yelled. "Where are you?"

"He's no on this level," Ryan's voice drifted down. "Cannae see him in any of the cages, neither."

The bottom door slowly opened. Oakley held his breath as the child inched in.

Holding his hand was a large black chimp.

"Found him," The teenager hissed. "But he's got company."

"Move away, Frankie." Siobhan was at the top of the stairs, rifle trained on the primate. "I don't want to hit you by mistake."

"Take a chance, doll." Ryan and Tyler appeared behind her. "Before Cheetah there rips the kid a new jaw."

"He won't hurt me." Frankie moved in front of the animal. "He's my friend."

"That's the chimp who protected me." Siobhan lowered her weapon. "This is beyond insane."

"His name is Satan." Oakley indicated the picture on the wall. "And he's in charge of the zoo now. Isn't that what you said earlier, Frankie?"

"Yes."

"Yah *think*?" Ryan moved to the top of the stairs. "I'll go doon and mess up that hairy wanker, right now."

"Let go of his hand." Oakley beckoned to the child. "If he's in charge, he caused this carnage. Killed all the humans."

The ape sniffed loudly.

"He knows what he did." The child hung his head. "But you're my friends too, so he's promised not to hurt any of you."

Dax kicked away the smouldering mattresses and sat up. The room was a blackened shell and flames were licking across the ceiling. A chunk of sheared off propeller protruded from one burning wall and she could see through the ruined quarters right out to Wilson Park, now a sea of fire. Pieces of roasted animal flesh stuck to shattered furniture.

"Mondo!" she screamed. "Where are you?"

"Over here."

"Thank God!" Dax pulled the smouldering mattresses away, uncovering the boy. She swallowed hard.

Mondo's face was red and puckered, clothes blackened and hair almost gone. He had dozens of bite marks inflicted by the creatures who had mauled him.

"Are they dead?" he wheezed through split lips.

"Every one of them."

"Excellent." The boy coughed loudly and a wad of crimson phlegm spilled from his mouth. "We best get going."

He tried to rise, then sank back with a whimper.

"I can't seem to move."

"I'll get help. Just lie there."

"More animals will find me long before that." Mondo closed his eyes. "I saw a medicine cabinet earlier."

"It's probably in the next county by now." Dax looked up. "Mondo, the building is burning."

"I just need a minute." He gritted bloody teeth. "Am I injured?"

"Not too badly." Dax lied.

"Can you lift me up? S'all right. I'm tough."

"I got you." She put a hand under his back and tried to pull him into a sitting position. There was a crunching sound and the girl quickly withdrew her hand.

It was soaked red.

"Did that hurt?"

"Can't feel a thing." Mondo tried to rise again. "Why is that, Dax?"

"I think your spine is broken."

"Oh." A tear trickled down the boy's cheek. "You should go then."

"I can carry you."

"You may as well shout 'dinner is served' when you head through the door."

"You're a funny guy." Dax searched for somewhere to gain purchase on Mondo's body that wasn't lacerated or burnt.

"I *am* very light." He closed his eyes. "Dax? Things are a bit misty. Am I dying?"

"Shhhhh." The girl gave up and held his hand. "I'm right here."

"I know." Mondo's head lolled to one side. "Like you promised."

"I'm really sorry for what I said earlier."

But Mondo was no longer listening. His eyes closed and he gradually stopped breathing.

Dax waited until she was sure the boy was dead. Then she let go and searched for the rifle. It had slipped down between the mattresses and was still intact.

A chink of flaming roof landed a few feet away. If she didn't leave now, the rest of the destroyed building would collapse on top of her.

Dax pulled the shard of propeller from the wall, climbed out of the bedroom window and dropped to the ground. There was no question of making a bee line for the ladder. The path was still slicked with flaming petrol and Wilson Park was impassable. She would have to detour south then work her way round.

She tried to remember the layout of the zoo. If she ran for the ape house and out the other side, she should just be able to circumvent the firestorm.

Dax set off at a trot.

Half way down the side path, a jaguar came racing towards her.

She didn't slow down. As the creature leapt, Dax swung the chunk of propeller up from her waist. The jagged edge sank into the creature's chest and almost burst out of its back.

"Devil in a dress, yeah?" The girl put her boot on the cat's body and pulled the weapon free. "I liked that, Mondo."

She stood in the middle of the inferno, dressed in black, holding the gory blade in one hand and her rifle in the other. Her hollow eyes shone brightly, through the mascara and blood streaking her face.

"I think hell suits me."

-35-

The teenagers backed slowly away from Satan.

"You seem to know a lot more than you're letting on, Frankie," Oakley whispered. "Want to try explaining?"

"You won't hurt me?"

"Depends what you say," Ryan spat. "Start by telling King Kong tae take a hike, before I lay intae him."

"He's been around humans his whole life. He understands you."

"Aw right." Ryan jerked a thumb towards the door. "Get lost, ugly. Before Tyler here removes yer monkey nuts."

"Go keep your tribe calm," Frankie whispered gently to the creature. "Oakley won't let anything happen to me."

Satan gestured at the child, tapping its fingers together.

"He says we have to leave soon. The fire is getting closer."

"You speak ape now?" Siobhan help up her camera phone and pressed record.

"He's using human sign language."

"How stupid of me."

219

"Let him through." The boy let go of Satan's hand. "I promise I'll explain everything."

The chimp blew the teenagers a loud raspberry and plodded up the stairs, Frankie trotting behind. The teenagers gave the creature a wide berth, but he simply grunted, unlocked the top door and vanished.

"Sit down." Oakley secured the door again and patted a bench. "Talk to us. We won't be mad."

"You promise?"

"I promise."

"How do you know sign language?"

"My mum showed me."

"Don't believe anything he says!"

"Dax?" Siobhan gasped.

The girl was limping up the stairs, rifle pointed at the little boy.

"For the love o God!" Ryan fumed. "Will somebody guard these doors? It's like Glasgow flyover at rush hour in here."

"Nothing's following me, yeah? There's a wall of fire between us and the other animals. I only just got through."

"You aw right, babe?" Tyler pulled a balled up tissue from his metal sleeve and tossed it to her. "You look like you've been dragged face doon through a slaughterhouse."

"Not far from the truth." Dax caught it, keeping the rifle trained on Frankie. "Oakley? Get away from him."

"Lower the gun." The boy got in front of his ward. "He's a little boy."

"He's a little *monster*."

"Frankie's the key to what's going on, Dax."

"I'm well aware of that." The girl clutched at the bannister, breathing heavily. "Do you know what me and Mondo found in the keepers' quarters?"

"Where *is* Mondo?" Siobhan asked, heart sinking. "Is he all right?"

"Died saving me, yeah?"

"Oh."

"We found a pair of child's pyjamas in the empty bed." Dax wiped blood from her face with the tissue.

"Frankie's been in the zoo all night."

"That true?" Oakley asked the child.

"Yes," Frankie said. "It is."

"But you told us you were on a school trip? Why lie about it?"

"So this wouldn't happen." The boy's eyes were glued to Dax's gun.

"Don't listen to him," the girl snarled. "He might look normal but he's changed, like the other animals. I bet he's much smarter and just as vicious as they are."

"Aw, wee man." Tyler sighed. "You cannae be my sidekick if you're a super villain."

"I'm not a baddie," Frankie retorted. "I tried to do what was right."

"Lower your gun, Dax." Oakley put his arm around the child. "Let's hear what he has to say. Please?"

"If I don't like it, I'm going to shoot him."

"Frankie, I'm trusting you. OK?" The teenager kissed his head.

"Exactly what happened last night?"

-Part 4-

Wild crows can recognise individual human faces and hold a grudge for years against people who have treated them badly. This ability – which may also exist in other wild animals – highlights how carefully some animals monitor the humans with which they share living space.

New Scientist

-36-

Sharon Rooney sat in the staff room of the ape enclosure, leafing through a sheaf of notes. Her son, Frankie, perched on a stool playing his Nintendo DS. Every now and then the boy's eyes darted to a large bag of Jelly Babies on the shelf next to him.

Dr Rupert Costello sat opposite Sharon, sipping a cup of coffee - a small man with round glasses and a wispy beard. Costello was an inspector for the World Health Organisation's Veterinary Public Health Department and his very presence worried her.

"Sorry to call you in at this hour," he slurped. "I didn't realise you were with your son."

"We've been at the movies."

"Ah. That's why I couldn't reach you earlier." Costello gave the boy a cheery wave, which Frankie ignored. "As head ape keeper, however, I thought you'd want to be here."

"What's wrong?"

225

"The test samples I took last month have been ana-lysed and, for the most part, your animals have a clean bill of health."

"For the most part?" Those certainly weren't words Sharon wanted to hear.

"Turns out the apes are carrying a mild strain of James Valley Fever virus."

"I'm afraid I'm not familiar with it."

"That's because it's extremely rare. And a good job too." Costello got up and poured himself more coffee. "Incredibly contagious. 80% fatality rate."

He sat down casually again as if he were discussing the weather.

"We only have a couple of human cases on record – both in the Congo in the 2000s. It didn't spread be-cause it killed all the infected villagers before they could get to other populations. A real nasty one."

"Human cases?" Sharon glanced apprehensively at Frankie, but the little boy didn't seem to be paying at-tention. "My son is here all the time."

"Relax, Mrs Rooney."

"It's Miss."

"This is a strain I haven't seen before but, as I said, it's very mild. It's not affecting the apes and it's no-where near zoonosis stage."

Zoonosis. Another word keepers dreaded. It meant the ability of a disease to jump from an animal species to human beings. Words like Aids, Ebola, Swine and Avian Flu sprang into Sharon's head. All were viruses that started off unique to animals but had eventually infected people.

"Are you sure?" she asked nervously.

"Don't worry," Costello grinned. "Tests indicate it's completely dormant. The virus would have to mutate massively before it could infect humans or even harm the apes. And it won't get that chance."

"That's why you're here?"

"Yes. The W.H.O. has developed a general antibiotic, which we've already used successfully in other zoos. It'll kill most primate diseases stone dead, and it's fast acting too. Only takes a couple of hours to flush the virus out of the apes' systems."

"I can get a team together to sedate the chimps. They don't like injections."

"Job's already done." Costello nodded at the bag on the shelf. "The antibiotic is infused into those Jelly Babies. They've already scoffed a box."

He looked contrite. "I would have consulted you first, but your mobile was turned off and I have a plane to catch."

"No, that's fine," Sharon said. "Jelly Babies. How ingenious."

"Apes love sweeties, as you know."

"I love sweeties too," Frankie mumbled, trying to look like he wasn't chewing.

"Did you eat any of those?" Sharon leapt up. "Spit them out right now!"

"I already swallowed," the boy gulped.

"Calm down, Ms Rooney." Costello smiled again. "It won't do him any harm."

He winked at the boy over the rim of his cup.

"I used to eat worms when I was your age."

"That's gross." But Frankie looked relieved.

"You sure it's safe?" Sharon asked.

"Have a couple if you like," Rupert Costello waved at the bag. "Though the green ones taste awful. Never saw the appeal in lime flavour."

"No thanks. The staff and I will take the regular injections tomorrow. I'm old fashioned."

"I'm afraid you'll have to stay here overnight," the vet continued. "In case any of the chimps has an allergic reaction. It's not going to happen, of course, but that's protocol for you." He took off his glasses and wiped steam from them with his tie.

"I took the liberty of sending one keeper home and putting you on the rota instead."

"Of course." Sharon turned to Frankie. "You ok sleeping in the keeper's quarters with me?"

"Yeah. I like the zoo."

"Wouldn't he rather stay with his dad?"

"His father died a couple of years ago."

"Oh. I didn't know."

Frankie looked down quickly, concentrating on his Nintendo.

"But you *will* have to empty the ape house tomorrow," Rupert Costello continued. "Give it a deep clean and disinfect the surrounding area."

"I'll get on that first thing." Sharon understood the instructions perfectly. The apes were now inoculated but the virus might live on for several hours in the warm droppings and straw strewn across the floor of their cages.

"Then I better catch my flight." Costello checked his watch. "Baby polar bear due to be born at Hamburg Zoo. I keep it alive and they're bound to name it after me."

"Rupert the bear?"

"How could they refuse?"

-37-

Sharon tucked Frankie up in bed, before getting undressed.

"See you in the morning, honey." She kissed his cheek.

"The other keepers snore," he grumped.

"So do you."

"Do not." The child pulled up his covers. "Can I see Rupert the Bear?"

"Not on my salary."

"Thought not. Night night, mum."

"Night baby."

Frankie woke in darkness, his head foggy. The alarm clock next to him read 3.10am. There was a strange glow coming from the window above his bed.

He opened it and leaned out.

A streak of pale luminescence sliced through the night sky and landed near the ape house. Frankie thought about fetching his mother, but she was always

231

irritated when he woke her. Instead, he snuggled back under the duvet and was asleep in seconds, leaving the window open.

When he awoke again, it was still dark. The clock said 5.00am.

Frankie felt different.

Thoughts he had never experienced before raced round and round his mind. Solutions to problems he hadn't even considered danced across his brain. His heart was pounding and his mouth dry. He forced himself to calm down.

Sums were his worst subject at school. He sat up and calculated.

$576 X 4768 = 2,746,368$. He had no doubt the answer was correct.

This was worth waking his mother for. He scampered over to her bed and prodded the sleeping woman.

"Mum?" He shook the prone form. "Something strange has happened to me!"

Sharon didn't stir. Frankie pulled the covers back.

His mother's eyes were rolled back in her head and a black tongue protruded from swollen lips.

"Mum?"

He felt for her pulse like he had seen doctors do on TV. There was none.

"Mummy?" He shook the woman harder.

But he already knew Sharon Rooney was gone. He checked the other keepers. They were dead too.

Frankie sat and howled until he couldn't cry any more. But even overwhelmed with grief, his mind was whirring as if it were some machine. There was something he needed to figure out. Something vital. Not even his mother's death could get in the way.

The child thought about last night. What Rupert Costello had said. Though he hadn't really been listening, he was able to remember every word.

The virus would have to mutate massively before it could infect humans or even harm the apes.

Tiny sparks and pinpoints of light swarmed in front of his eyes, as he considered a million possibilities at once. Then he padded through to the computer in the staff room and Googled 'James River Fever'.

James River Fever is an extremely rare and virulent viral <u>zoonosis</u>, which can kill within 48 hours. Symptoms include red blotches on the skin which resemble insect bite marks.

Frankie rubbed his face. He ran through every permutation of what might have happened and settled on the only explanation possible.

The virus in the ape house had obviously infected his mum and the other night keepers. But it shouldn't have *harmed* them.

Unless it had, somehow… changed.

That had to be the reason. And the altered strain was more deadly than the worst James Valley Virus outbreaks Rupert Costello had described. This time the disease had killed its hosts within a few hours, not two days. He was only alive because, like the chimps, he had eaten inoculated Jelly Babies.

But what could suddenly turn a harmless virus into a virulent contagion?

The light in the sky.

He thought about the anime programmes he loved to watch. In one, an asteroid had landed on earth and caused anyone who came near it to evolve into flesh eating monsters. But that was just a *cartoon*.

Still, it was all he had to go on. He began to Google again, looking up *asteroids*.

There were several reports about a recent cluster of meteors named the TH4X group. They had been monitored approaching the planet, but none were deemed a threat, according to the meteorological office. Three fragments had actually entered the earth's atmosphere, without making the national news.

He looked up the locations where the fragments had been predicted to land. The first was near Birjand, Turkmenistan. The second was in the Atlantic Ocean off the Newfoundland coast. The third, the Scottish highlands.

A horrible idea began to scratch at the corners of his mind. He Googled *strange occurrences near Birjand, Turkmenistan.*

And there it was.

Rumours of cannibal children in the desert

Reports have surfaced of feral children rampaging through a village near Birjand, Turkmenistan. According to local tribesmen, the children had 'turned into monsters' and begun killing the villagers. They then attacked a squad of heavily armed British soldiers sent to investigate.

The tribesmen claimed the tragedy happened after a 'strange light' was seen descending from the sky.

A British Army spokesman described the reports as 'complete fabrication'.

"Fabrication my bum."

Another search revealed a Port Cresta trawler missing near the coast of Newfoundland. A Royal Navy destroyer had been diverted to the area and joined in the search. Frankie gave a sort of derision. After discovering what had happened at Birjand, he was certain the British forces weren't looking for survivors. They were searching for the second meteor fragment.

He was willing to bet the third hadn't come down in the highlands, as predicted, but landed in Edinburgh Zoo. It had somehow changed him and he was pretty certain it had altered the James River Virus as well. What it might have done to the other animals wasn't something he wanted to dwell on.

The military would come hunting for that too, unaware of how deadly it really was.

Frankie thought hard.

He and the chimps had been inoculated, so they were safe from the disease and unable to pass it on. The night keepers were dead and there were no other people in the zoo. Dr Costello said James River Fever was unique to chimps and humans. Hopefully, the other denizens of the zoo were immune to the disease and he could discount them as carriers.

The virus was contained for now. It might be lingering in the dirt and faeces of the ape house but, with no hosts left to spread the contagion, it would die out in a few hours.

Unless more people turned up. And not just the army.

Frankie looked at his watch. The morning shift would be arriving soon, then the visitors. They would never believe a seven-year-old boy with a theory he'd gotten from a cartoon. But, if one person picked up the virus and ventured into a heavily populated area, it could turn into a pandemic.

He had to prevent people entering the zoo for as long as possible. Somehow, he *must* keep everyone away. There must be a way to *make* the authorities cordon off the place.

He picked up the phone, dialled 999 and asked for police, lowering his voice to sound like an adult. Despite his best efforts, he sounded more female than male.

"Listen carefully," he said. "I have released a deadly virus at Edinburgh Zoo. It's very contagious."

The police operator at the other end sounded tired and grumpy.

And I know a hoax when I hear it.

"Trace the call. You'll see I'm phoning from the zoo. It's the same virus that altered the children at Birjand, Turkmenistan. Look it up on the web."

Listen. I've taken enough prank calls in the past to fill a log book. This line is for real emergencies, not morons trying to impress their mates with a stupid dare.

"No. Wait! There's going to be carnage if you don't…"

Yeah, yeah. Next week you'll be warning me about an alien invasion.

The policeman hung up.

Frankie slammed the phone down. Stupid cop! How would he keep people away now?

A horrible plan began to form in his mind. But it was all he had.

The child got dressed. He gathered up all the keys in the night keeper's quarters, let himself out, and made his way to ape house. On the way, he passed a dozen other enclosures, red eyes regarding him balefully from the darkness. None of the other animals had died from an infection, which only backed up his wild hypothesis.

He had no choice but to let them free. Once the keepers arrived and found the creatures loose, the authorities would seal the place up and stop anyone entering the zoo. It would give the James River Fever time to die out and he could try and find the fragment before the army arrived.

Satan had his face pressed against the glass when the child entered. Because his mum was the head keeper, they were familiar with each other. Frankie was even allowed to feed the primate treats. Now there was an awareness in the animal's eyes he had never seen before.

Satan knew a few words of sign language Sharon Rooney had taught him. Nothing complicated. *Yes. No. I want.* Despite repeated attempts, it was all he'd ever learned. Yet, when Frankie entered, the ape began to sign frantically.

Let me out. Let me out.

"Can you understand me?" The child asked.

Yes.

It seemed as if Satan was smarter too. If so, he suspected all the animals might be. Like the James River Virus, they had somehow *evolved* overnight.

"Will you hurt me if I set you free?"

Humans bad. The chimp shook its matted head. *You good. You friend.*

"Will you help me?"

I help. What I do?

"I'm setting you loose." Frankie unlocked the cage, letting Satan witness exactly what he was doing. When the chimp cautiously emerged, he pressed the keys into the creature's hand.

"Did you see how I unlocked the door?"

Yes.

"Do the same with all the other cages."

-38-

"That's my story." Frankie looked dolefully at the teenagers clustered round him. "Now you know everything.

"Sorry about your mum," Tyler pulled a face. "But you've been a naughty wee scamp, eh?"

"Naughty!" Ryan exploded. "The wee shit got everyone killed."

"That's not fair!" Frankie retorted. "The zoo was still empty at that time of the morning. When the day keepers arrived and saw the animals loose, I was sure they'd seal the place off and call the police."

"So what went wrong, Frankie?" Oakley purposely kept his voice calm and steady. "Why did Satan wait till visitors arrived before unlocking the cages?"

"No. He and the other apes did what I said right away." The boy was a picture of misery. "Only they left the gates *closed*. Everything looked fine when the staff arrived, so they had breakfast before they did their morning rounds. By that time visitors were already coming in."

Frankie looked at Oakley sorrowfully.

"I didn't realise at first. I swear."

"Where *were* you?" Dax snarled. "Playing your bloody Nintendo?"

"Trying to find the stupid meteor fragment," the child said defiantly. "It's responsible for changing me and all the other living things here. I'm still trying to work out what else it might do."

"How convenient."

"If all the creatures were smarter," Oakley pondered. "Didn't they realise they were free?"

"Oh, they did. But, instead of coming out, they *waited*." The boy rubbed his tiny hands together miserably. "They wanted to kill as many people as they could. And the apes showed them the best way. They hate humans as much as the other animals. Maybe more."

"That's no very sociable, is it?" Tyler scratched his head. "We feed them an clean oot their poo."

"They're finally clever enough to realise they're caged. So they killed their guards and punished the people who came to gape at them. Wouldn't you do the same, if you were incarcerated for no reason?"

"They're just animals!" Oakley protested.

"So are we."

"Kiddie's not wrong," Tyler shrugged. "Just look at oor estate."

"We don't lock people up if they're not too bright, do we?" Frankie thumped on the glass of the cage. "Why aren't they treated with the same courtesy?"

"They murdered our friends." Siobhan reminded him. "Don't you *dare* defend them."

"And how many hamburgers have each of us had in the last week?"

"About fifteen," Tyler admitted.

"Why didn't they escape the zoo, altogether?" Oakley asked gently. "If they wanted revenge, there's a whole housing complex next door they could have gone after."

"They may be brighter, but their instincts haven't changed," Frankie replied. "This is the only territory they know, so they won't go outside it. Instead, they'll defend it to the death."

"They're a big gang now." Tyler nodded sagely. "This is their turf and we're in the middle o it."

"Save the animal rights debate for yir next Greenpeace meetin, and let's cut tae the chase," Ryan fumed. "Curious George oot there seems tae have finally switched sides. Will he help us get tae safety?"

"No. He still hates humans. But he won't stop you either."

"Why not?

"He owes me for freeing him and doesn't want to repay me by killing any more of my friends. That's why he spared Siobhan."

"You still think we're pals? Cause *I've* totally gone aff you."

"Give him a break, eh?" Oakley snapped. "He might be a genius but he's only seven. He did what he thought was right."

"*You* should understand that, Ry." Tyler scolded. "Where we come fae, you join the local crew or you're a dead man."

"If the James River Virus infected just one person and they made it out of the zoo, it would start an epidemic." Frankie got behind Oakley. "I'm talking thousands dead. Maybe hundreds of thousands."

The teenagers looked at each other.

"I risked my own life to try and contain the disease." The child pressed home his advantage. "Gave up searching for the rock, looked for survivors and gave them Jelly Babies."

"Hey," Ryan interrupted. "We didnae get any Jelly Babies."

"Do you feel ill?"

"Nah. Neither does Tyler."

"I'm fine, apart fae a touch of indigestion." The boy burped. "Must be aw those hot dogs."

"Then, hopefully, the virus has already burned itself out."

"Great! Let's get the hell out of here."

"Can Satan order the other animals to let us past, at least?" Oakley asked. "You said he was in charge of the zoo."

"Only when he was directing them to kill people. They'll see him as a traitor for not getting rid of us too.

He's having trouble keeping his own tribe under control." The child's shoulders drooped. "You still have to fight your way out."

"Fine by me." Ryan patted his sword. "Any lion comes near? I'll turn him intae kitty nibbles."

"We do have to leave, yeah?" Dax reluctantly agreed. "The fire is getting closer."

"Not me." Frankie folded thin arms. "The meteor fragment is still here and I'm not going without it. The military must be desperate to get their hands on it, after what they saw in Birjand. Think of what a weapon it would make."

"They could use it to make super soldiers," Oakley nodded. "That must be why the army were all on manoeuvres in the highlands. It was a cover so they could look for the other fragment. Now they've realised it came down in the zoo instead."

"You played right into their hands, Frankie," Siobhan said. "I bet they used your phone call to persuade everyone that terrorists had caused a plague here. It gave them a perfect excuse to quarantine the place."

"I know. For a genius, I've been pretty stupid." Frankie sighed. "As far as I could see from the internet posts, the area around Birjand is pretty much made of rocks. And the second meteor landed in the ocean. This is their last chance and, I imagine, they'll go to any lengths to secretly retrieve it."

He tugged his ear.

"They won't want us alive to tell the real story, either."

"Why not let them find their precious rock?" Dax suggested. "If we can sneak out of the zoo and stay mum, they'll be none the wiser."

"Why *aren't* you smarter?" the boy asked. "Like the animals?"

"Don't push it shorty. I'm no dummy."

"If the meteor was *still* mutating organic material, you'd *all* be geniuses by now." The boy raised his hands in exasperation. "But you're not, so it isn't."

He tapped his head. "Why is that? Think."

The teenagers considered this.

"We don't know."

"*Something* triggered a burst of energy from the fragment. Activated it, if you like. I'm guessing it was the heat of descending through the atmosphere."

"So what?"

"Suppose the military subject it to extreme heat again?"

"Let them. From what I've seen, the army could do with a few more brains."

"This thing causes rapid evolution in living tissue," Frankie said patiently as if explaining to a child his age. "Imagine one of the scientists working on the project having a cold. It could mutate into another disease. One that might wipe out every creature on earth."

There was silence.

"Cannae let that happen, Ryan." Tyler sounded suitably alarmed. "Mah gran gets terrible flu every winter, as it is. She cannae afford to heat her flat properly."

"This ape house was the focal point of the James River Virus," the boy said pointedly. "I could have destroyed any remaining traces of the disease, and solved all our problems, by simply burning it down. But I can't subject the meteor to *heat*."

He began to cry.

"Honestly. It's right around here somewhere. Only I'll never find it. Like you said, it's just a lump of stone and there are millions scattered about. I don't even have a Geiger counter."

He wiped his eyes. "But I've got to try, don't you see? There's a *fire* coming. Heat will set it off again."

"Just ask the monkey, you wee moron," Ryan said acidly.

"Apes aren't nocturnal. They were asleep when the meteor came down."

"So what? If Satan's been stuck in here for years, he must be bored enough tae count every rock in this place. He'd easily suss out a new one."

Frankie stared at the teenager.

"That's brilliant."

"And I didnae need a bolt from the sky. Just a wee bit o common sense."

Frankie led the chimp back into the enclosure, holding its hand. Dax blanched, finger tightening on the trigger of her rifle.

"Let it be." Siobhan pushed the gun up. "We need him, for now."

What is different? Frankie signed, curling his fingers into a fist. *A rock. A new rock.*

The ape looked around.

Same. It gestured back sadly. *Always same.*

"Jeez." Oakley looked ashamed. "His life's more boring than mine."

No. Outside. Frankie coaxed. The chimp climbed the tree in its cage and scanned the area.

There! New rock. He was pointing to the sea lion enclosure outside. In the middle was an artificial island with a concrete beach.

"Which one does he mean?" Siobhan groaned. "There are loads of stones."

"Can you send him to get the right one?"

"Apes don't swim very well."

"One of us will have to go." Oakley pressed his face against the glass. "Where are the sea lions, Frankie?"

"They were shipped to another zoo a few days ago as part of a breeding programme."

"A lucky break at last." Siobhan checked her rifle. There were three bullets left in the chamber. "That rock's our proof of what the army is up to. We have to find it."

"You can't use it as part of your story!" The child tugged at her sleeve. "We need to hide it where it'll never be found."

"You think?" The girl shook him off. "That's still up for discussion."

-39-

The lid of a garbage bin creaked open and Brandon peeked out. Further down the hill, he could see soldiers in the estate running from house to house.

"As if I'd be dumb enough to trap myself there," he chuckled, climbing out and dusting himself off. "Got to start finding less smelly places to hide, though."

His next move was obvious. The north side of the zoo was ringed by thick woods. He could move through the trees undetected until he was far enough away to be safe. By the time anyone found his skateboard in the trash, he'd be long gone.

He crept into the undergrowth and began to walk, keeping his head low, ready to dive for cover. He felt bad about the other kids but there wasn't any way to warn them. He had to think of himself. If Sandy were still alive, it might have been different. She was the sort of girl who would insist on staying to help.

He didn't like to think about that.

Brandon heard a noise to his right and crouched down. People were talking in whispers and he could hear muted sobbing.

Leave it be, he said to himself. *Don't get involved.*

Curiosity got the better of him. He crawled towards the sounds and parted the bushes. A small dirt track separated him from two strangers attempting to get into the zoo.

A man stood against the wall, with a dark haired woman perched precariously on his shoulders. She was crying and trying to reach the barbed wire on top.

"Can you get it honey?" the man urged. "Stretch as high as you can."

"I'm not tall enough," the woman cried. "Stand on your toes. Please!"

"I already am. Can't hold your weight like this much longer."

The woman gave a small jump, her hand brushing the wire.

Brandon winced. Even if she managed to grab it, the barbs would slice through her flesh. The man gave a groan and sank down an inch, unbalancing his partner. She toppled backwards and landed awkwardly, sprawling across the ground.

In an instant, she was on her feet and clambering up the man's back again. It was obvious they weren't going to breach the defences, but they kept trying.

Brandon considered showing himself, then thought better of it. Even if *he* stood on the man's shoulders and the woman climbed on his, there was no way she could get over those vicious, rusted loops.

A police car rounded the corner, skidded to a halt and two officers with shotguns got out. Seeing the couple were no threat, they tossed the weapons back into the car and advanced. Brandon slid lower until he was simply a pair of eyes, peeping through the mass of leaves.

"Sir? Madam?" one officer shouted. "You know the zoo is quarantined."

"Our daughter is in there," the man yelled back. "She was at an award ceremony."

Brandon groaned silently.

"There's nothing you can do," the other policeman said stolidly. "There's a plague alert. We have orders to escort everyone to a safe distance."

"Look. Look!" The woman pulled a photograph and held it out. "This is her. Just let us try. I'm begging you."

"We're willing to take the chance of not coming out again," the man joined in. "We could climb on your car roof and get over that way."

He clasped his hands together. "We just want to help her. Her name's Dax Martin. She's only fifteen!"

Dax! Brandon bit his lip until it bled.

"Please," he whispered to himself. "Ignore your orders for once!"

The first PC glanced at his companion but the man shook his head sadly.

"We can't." His voice was ragged. "It's a matter of national security." He moved towards the couple. "I'm truly sorry, but you need to get in the vehicle with us."

Dax's father turned and ran, dragging his wife behind him. The police gave chase, rapidly gaining on the couple. One wrestled the man to the ground and the other pinned the woman's arms behind her back, reaching for his handcuffs.

"No. No. I'm not having this." Brandon broke cover and sprinted for the car.

"There are kids still alive in there, you assholes!" he bellowed at the astonished policemen. "I'll do your damned job for you, will I?"

He jumped inside, started the engine and roared off.

"Lucky my brother taught me to drive, eh Sandy?" He picked up speed, leaving the cursing officers in his wake. "Time to pull off another mental ride."

He grasped the wheel tightly, hands steady, as they always were when he did something stupid.

"This time I really will make you proud."

-40-

Yellow Leader gathered his men in a huddle. Above them, one chopper had winched away the tree blocking the entrance and was about to lift the ruined Armed Response Vehicle. Soldiers were loading guns into a second abandoned ARV.

"The housing estate is cordoned off," a sergeant shouted over the whine of the rotors. "We haven't located the boy yet, but he must be in there somewhere."

"Shoot him on sight," Yellow Leader commanded. "Say he was heading for the evacuees and it was the only way to stop him."

He gave a heartfelt sigh.

"Guererro already fired on him. If he gets away, he'll probably point that fact out and we'll be up for war crimes."

"I'll get it done, Sir."

"Red Leader. You and your men take over patrolling the perimeter. Anyone comes over that wall, you know what to do." He shook his head wearily. "Once our main force gets here, they can go in en masse and find the meteor. After that, it's up to top brass to convince the public that we genuinely thought there was a terrorist threat."

There was a loud metallic groan, as the crushed ARV was lifted into the air and dumped unceremoniously into a ditch.

"My men will take the second Armed Response vehicle into the zoo and scout around," Yellow Leader said. "It's built like a tank. Even a rhino wouldn't dent it, as long as it doesn't knock over another tree."

"Will do, Sir."

A police car skidded round the corner and made for the entrance, accelerating rapidly.

"What the hell is the driver up to?" The soldiers ran towards it, waving their arms. The vehicle didn't stop. The men threw themselves out of the way as it shot past.

"Land that chopper, now!" Yellow Leader yelled into his walkie talkie. "Before he reaches the gate!"

The helicopter descended, wind from its rotors whipping up a maelstrom of dust. The police car scraped underneath, bounced into the zoo and slewed to a halt.

Brandon got out, carrying a shotgun. He took aim and blew away the chopper's tail blades.

"It's the boy!" Yellow Leader sighted his own weapon. "How in God's name did..."

Before he could finish his sentence, the chopper landed with a thump, wrecking the undercarriage. Brandon leaned round the side and blew them a kiss. Then he got back in the panda car and vanished into the zoo interior.

"Quite a feat, kid." Yellow Leader gave a low whistle. Despite his frustration, he couldn't help admiring the teen's bravado. "We're going to have to pursue you."

"But now our *helicopter* is blocking the entrance, Sir. And it has the only winch."

"Then we'll proceed on foot."

His men looked at each other.

"That's suicide," one said hesitantly. "Look what happened to the cops."

"Besides, he won't stand a chance in there," another added. "If the animals don't get him, the fire will."

"He got out once, didn't he?" Yellow Leader retorted. "This debacle is beginning to attract worldwide attention. We have to make sure everyone in there is dead before the smoke clears and every spy satellite in the sky starts pointing at the place."

He checked his gun and unfastened a respirator from his belt. "Masks on, so we can maintain our cover story. They'll protect us from the fumes as well."

He waved his men away.

"We'll say we attempted a rescue mission, even though we had no transport. Play our cards right and we may even come out of this looking like heroes."

-41-

The teenagers stood at the edge of the sea lion pool. Satan's tribe were perched on the roof of the ape enclosure, staring despondently into the distance. The leader signalled to Frankie.

"He says the other animals are moving through the zoo," the boy translated. "They're going north eastward before the fire traps them."

"We'll be in the same boat soon." Siobhan nodded at the broiling clouds polluting the air. "We can't have long."

"One problem at a time, eh?" Ryan dipped a metal toe in the water. "This pond's full o green stuff."

"Aye," Tyler said. "Who exactly is gonnae go fetch the meteor thingie?"

"I... eh... can't swim." Oakley looked embarrassed.

"I'm no too great in water myself." Ryan banged his breastplate. "Wearin this, I'd go down like a priest in a knockin shop."

"I dinnae even like takin a bath," Tyler added.

"Hell. I'll get it, yeah?" Dax began unzipping her boots. "I could do with washing off this soot."

"I thought that was just your mascara, toots."

"The pool hasn't been cleaned since the sea lions left." Frankie pointed to a rip in the girl's jeans, crusted with dried blood. "If bacteria gets into a gash in your leg, it'll infect it for sure. You'd need shots and you can't exactly go to a doctor."

"I hadn't noticed." Dax looked down and, for the first time, her voice softened towards the child. "Thank you."

"I suppose it's muggins here who's in for a dunking." Siobhan kicked off her own boots, then pulled down her skirt and tights. "No laughing when my makeup washes away. I've got freckles and I'm a bit self-conscious about them."

Frankie handed over his backpack. Siobhan put it on and gingerly entered the water.

"It's freezing! Still, I'm a good swimmer. I did a course in life saving, in case I had to cover a sinking ship. Never thought being an overachiever would come in so handy."

She plunged, head first, into the dirty water and swam to the island. Pulling herself onto dry land, she started picking up small boulders and holding them aloft for Satan to inspect.

"This one?"

The ape waved her further on.

"This one? This?"

That way. Satan indicated.

"Warmer? This one?"

The chimp held up three fingers.

"One… two… three." Siobhan stepped over more boulders. "This the guy?"

Satan nodded excitedly.

"That wasn't too hard." She dropped the rock into Frankie's rucksack and began to wade back. "Now all we have to do is get past an inferno, rabid animals and probably the British Army."

"Watch out for that log coming up behind!" Oakley shouted.

On the roof of the ape house, the chimps began to leap up and down, screeching and waving their arms in the air.

"What's wrong with them?" Siobhan froze. "Why are they acting like that?"

"It's not a log." Frankie went white. "That's an alligator!"

"Move, Siobhan!" Dax yelled. "It's right behind you!"

Siobhan glanced round at the shape gliding towards her, shrugged off the rucksack and threw it towards the shore. It bobbed on the surface, the air inside preventing it from sinking. Then the girl broke into a powerful crawl, arms and legs churning up dirty white foam.

A second ridged spine slid out from under an overhanging tree and made to cut her off.

"Dammit!" Oakley cursed. "There's *another* one."

"That's a crocodile," Frankie corrected. "His name is Munchy."

"Not the time, Chaz."

"Head for that outcrop!" Dax yelled.

A flat stone mound, made for the sea lions to sunbathe on, projected from the water just to Siobhan's left. The girl reached it and crawled onto the algae covered surface.

"Stay there, doll!" Ryan and Tyler waded into the pool, up to their knees. "We'll take care o this."

They repeatedly slammed gloved hands on the surface of the water. The crocodile detected the motion, changed direction and headed towards them. Dax took careful aim and fired at the alligator circling the outcrop.

"It's armour plated," Frankie said. "You have to hit the eyes."

"Do I look like William bloody Tell?" Dax loosed off another shot. "I'm doing my best, yeah?"

"Dinnae let me doon, Ty." Ryan moved deeper, on a collision course with the croc. "That scaly bugger's nae match for you, big man."

He took a deep breath as the alligator opened its mouth and clamped brutal jaws on his iron clad arm.

The creature reversed, pulling the boy with him. Ryan lost his footing and vanished below the waves.

Bellowing with rage, Tyler threw himself on top of the leviathan, hacking with his sword. Within seconds, all three combatants were submerged and the filthy water began to bubble and turn red. The apes were still screaming from the rooftop.

"C'mon you two!" Dax ran back and forth impotently along the water line. "You can take that giant handbag."

The waves began to settle.

"How many more are we going to lose?" Oakley bowed his head. "I thought those morons had charmed lives."

Tyler's head broke out of the water, gulping for air. Dax gave a shriek and clapped her hands.

The teenager forged his way back to the bank, dragging Ryan behind him. Beside them, the croc slowly rose to the surface, its soft underside sliced to pieces by the larger boy's blade.

"Think yir tough, eh?" Ryan spluttered at the dead beast. "I've mugged grannies who put up a better fight!"

He suddenly looked sheepish.

"Ehm... Forget I said that."

Siobhan was still perched, shivering, on top of the outcrop. The alligator circled lazily around her and, for the first time, they noticed it had spines on its back, rather than ridges.

"Come and have a go, if you think yir hard enough!" Tyler began to beat on the water again. He looked desperately at Dax.

"It's no movin towards me! I cannae go any deeper or I'll drown."

But the gator wasn't going to make the mistake of tackling iron clad adversaries. Finding the gentlest slope, it began to crawl onto the miniature island, snapping at the terrified girl. Siobhan stood up and prepared to dive.

"I'm going in." Dax handed her rifle to Frankie. "She can't swim faster than that beast."

"What's that noise?" The boy spun round. "It sounds like…"

A police car careened through the bushes and bumped across the concrete, sending up a shower of sparks. It stopped and Brandon Golledge emerged. In each hand, he held a strange shaped gun.

"Do exactly as I tell you, Siobhan!" he yelled splashing into the pond. "Stay where you are."

"Brandon?" The girl's tear streaked eyes widened in astonishment. "Is that you?"

"Don't dive!" The boy was already up to his waist, pistols held above his head. "Stand right in the centre of the rock!"

The alligator had hauled itself further up the outcrop, inches from Siobhan's feet. Spotting Brandon, however, it slid back into the water and headed for him.

"Grab that rucksack while you're out there, mate," Ryan urged. "We need it!"

"Never mind the damned bag," Dax yelled. "Get out of there! Bullets won't dent its armour!"

"Not using bullets, Dax." Brandon scooped up the rucksack and pointed his weapons.

"Get back from the edge of the pond!" Oakley gasped. "He's carrying Tasers!"

The boy waited until the beast was a few feet away and pulled both triggers.

Four wires streamed from the barrels of his weapons and hit the half submerged creature. There was a deafening bang and it burst into flames. Siobhan threw back her head, then collapsed on the rock.

10,000 volts of electricity surged through the water and fried Brandon. He toppled forwards and sank under the waves, taking the rucksack with him.

"Yir luck finally ran oot, blondie," Ryan said sadly. "Good effort, though."

"That was some stunt." Tyler removed his helmet. "Saved Siobhan's bacon, right enough."

He glanced at the prone figure on the rock.

"Who's gonna get her now?"

"Looks like the kiddie's takin care of business," Ryan pointed. "Nobody asked if *he* could swim."

Frankie was streaking through the water towards the outcrop, pulling Oakley along in his wake. The teenager had found a plank of wood and was doing an awkward doggie paddle in an effort to stay afloat.

"If they're sorted, let's check the car. That's our way oot, pal."

The pair ran over to the police vehicle and began rummaging inside.

Frankie and Oakley reached Siobhan, lying unconscious on the flat stone.

"She's OK." Frankie felt her pulse. "She was out of the water, so the electric shock she got wasn't nearly as bad as Brandon's."

As if on cue, Siobhan's eyes fluttered open.

"I ache all over." She gently touched her temple and winced. "Where's Brandon?"

"He's… ehm… I…"

"Where *is* he?"

Siobhan blinked rapidly, willing her eyes to focus. On the shore, Dax was sitting staring at the water.

"Where's Brandon, Dax?"

She looked across at them and sadly shook her head.

-42-

Frankie stood disconsolately at the edge of the pond, scanning the surface.

"The fragment's on the bottom, under ten feet of filthy water and there's absolutely no way for us to find it." Oakley put his arm around the child. "We'll just have to hope the army can't either."

A few yards away, Ryan and Tyler were inspecting Brandon's stolen car.

"We got two Remington 870 shotguns with a dozen cartridges." Ryan finished his inventory. "Couple more Tasers. A Glock 17 self-loading pistol and two Heckler and Koch G36 semi-automatic rifles." The boy looked impressed. "Blondie must have stopped and picked them up fae the dead firearms officers."

"How come you're such an expert on guns?" Oakley gaped, wringing water out of his hooded top.

"You dinnae want tae know."

"And he left the keys in the ignition," Tyler jingled them. "We got wheels."

"I've been learning to drive." Dax grabbed them from the boy. "Can we all fit inside?"

"Pop open the boot and me and Tyler will sit in it. Bit of rear-guard action, eh?" Ryan beckoned to Siobhan. "C'mon doll. We're offski."

Siobhan was crouched in a spreading puddle, staring at her mobile.

"I forgot to leave it on the shore." She held up the ruined device, water dripping from its casing. "Everything I recorded is lost."

"That's tough, toots." Tyler beckoned to her. "But we need tae leave. I'll stick the heatin on so you dinnae catch yir death o cold."

"Aye, you can die gettin chewed tae bits instead," Ryan said. "Like the rest o us."

"What about heading for the entrance now?" Oakley asked. "If the animals are gone, maybe we could beat the fire and get out that way."

"I don't think so." Frankie ran his hand along a row of holes in the car door. "Looks like the army was shooting at Brandon. I think we should head for the ladder."

"Me too." Ryan caressed the assault rifle lovingly. "We've got a ride and we're armed tae the teeth."

"And every animal in the zoo is heading north to escape the inferno," Oakley reminded them. "Wiped out the last people carrying these guns and *they* were trained officers."

"We cannae stay here, bud," Ryan coughed. "What about you, Dax? Entrance or ladder, like Frankie suggested?"

"I still don't trust that little creep." The girl curled her lip. "His mother died last night but he seemed more concerned about hiding a damned rock."

There was a horrified silence.

"That's a bit harsh, darlin," Ryan whispered. "I didnae think you'd go *there*."

"All right," she said reluctantly. "Ladder."

"And I don't care." Siobhan was hunched over, utterly defeated. "Not anymore."

Frankie tapped her on the shoulder. "If you still want proof that the animals are mutations, rather than plague carriers, it's in the zebra paddock."

"What are you talking about?" Siobhan raised her head.

"That guy, Bangles? He had a video camera."

"He had *what*?"

"In the Land Rover, he told me he'd recorded the zebras and gazelles killing his friend. Said they were all weird looking, with too many horns and teeth."

"He did mention that," Oakley backed the boy up. "It slipped my mind cause I was busy trying to keep my head attached to my neck."

"Where's the video recorder now?" Siobhan demanded.

"He left it up a tree in the zebra paddock."

"I want it." The girl stood up. "We're going for the ladder."

They began to climb into the car, but Frankie paused and looked up. The apes were still gathered on the roof of the enclosure.

"What's stopping the monkeys leaving?" Siobhan glanced at their silhouettes, outlined against the red sky. "I bet they could scramble over any part of the wall."

"That was their original idea," Frankie said. "The other animals are too territorial to leave but they're much smarter. They were going to escape into the woods during the confusion."

"But the trees only go on for a few hundred yards," Oakley said. "Then there's a quarry and more houses."

"They didn't know that until they were released from their cages and could see further," the child explained. "They'd never been out of the zoo."

"So they're just going to *sit* there?"

"That's their curse." He turned and walked away. "They're intelligent enough to know they're doomed."

"Where are you going?" Dax slapped her forehead, leaving a pale handprint in the grime and gore.

"To say goodbye."

"We don't have bloody time for that!"

"So, go without me." The child didn't look back. "That's what you want, anyway."

"I didn't…"

"Five minutes, Frankie." Oakley tapped his wrist. "It's all we can spare."

-43-

They sat in the car, waiting. Ryan and Tyler were folded uncomfortably in the boot, metal legs almost touching the ground. Siobhan lay in the back, holding her aching head. Oakley fidgeted in the front seat while Dax tested the controls.

"Think I should put the siren on?"

"Think I should walk up to a lion and stick my head in its mouth?" Siobhan snapped. "Save you the trouble of getting me killed."

"I was joking, yeah?"

"Somebody go an hurry that wee toerag up!" Ryan shouted. "I'm losing aw the feeling in mah bum."

"I'll get him before the apes throw the little trouble-maker off the roof." Dax pushed open the door. "They're probably as sick of him as me."

When the girl emerged onto the top of the ape house, Frankie had both arms around Satan, dishev-elled head pressed against his chest. The chimp rested one hand gently on the child's back in response. Dax stood a few feet away, eyeing the other primates with undisguised suspicion.

A female shuffled forwards and crouched next to the girl.

"That's close enough, Bubbles," Dax warned, stroking her rifle.

"Her name's Cecelia." Frankie finally let Satan go. "She's pregnant."

"Congratulations."

The ape rubbed her distended stomach proudly, black eyes sparkling.

"The chimp with the scar is called Otto," Frankie continued. "He's the joker. Ben is the serious one. Susan and Dirk are just babies, really."

The apes grinned and hooted as the child spoke their names.

"You trying to persuade them to come with us?" Dax asked archly. "They can get over the wall while we're being slaughtered."

"They want to try and escape, but Satan won't let them."

The chimps looked sorrowfully at their leader.

"Why not?"

"Only the youngsters are left. They don't really understand what will happen to them when they're recaptured. And they *will* be recaptured."

Their leader gave a sniff and stared longingly at the woods.

"But Satan has been around humans a long time." Frankie patted the hoary head and reluctantly turned away. "He knows they'll either be experimented on or spend the rest of their lives hidden on some secret base in a cage. Either fate is bad enough for a dumb animal. For creatures as aware as these, it would be torture."

"So is hanging around until they burn to death."

"I know." The child nodded to a pile of tranquilliser darts near Satan's feet. "So I brought him those. He knows exactly what they do."

"Frankie!" Dax inched towards the pile. "We need all the ammo we can get our hands on."

Satan bared his teeth at her.

"Good luck taking them back. We have plenty of other firepower."

"I *really* hate you, kid."

"Leave them some dignity, Dax." Frankie took the girl's hand. "They've only just discovered it."

He led her away, watched by a dozen pairs of anguished eyes.

"Now it's all they have left."

The pair quietly descended the stairs

"I didn't mean that crack about your mum," the girl apologised. "Well… I did. But I was furious."

"That's all right." Frankie stopped. "Dax, while we're alone, I have to tell you something."

"Is this going to make me angry again?"

"Yes. But you have to keep it to yourself."

"Am I the only one who sees how bloody manipulative you are?"

"Probably."

"Out with it, then."

"Ryan and Tyler didn't eat any Jelly Babies, so they're not immune to the James River Fever." The child picked at his lip. "And they were in the ape house for ages. It's the most likely place any microbes might still be hanging on."

"They don't seem ill." Dax thought back.

"Ryan is, but he's been trying to hide it," Frankie insisted. "Tyler knows there's something wrong with his pal, but he's pretending it's not happening."

Nothing gets past you, eh?"

"If Ryan is infected and *does* escape, then everything we've gone through will have been for nothing."

"Don't you *dare* try to stop him!" the girl snapped. "He saved our asses."

"How could I? He's wearing armour and I'm only seven."

"So you want me to do it?" She grabbed the boy by the collar. "You're asking me to stop him? Is that what you're saying?"

"I'm telling you the situation," the child choked. "That's all."

"Why dump this on me?" Dax pushed him away and he landed on his back. "Why not tell your good buddy, Oakley?"

"He's too nice to do anything about it," the boy said timidly, picking himself up. "You're not."

"I should have shot you earlier." Dax glanced at her rifle. "Still could."

"My friends on that roof are willing to sacrifice *themselves* because anything else is too terrible to contemplate." the boy said. "And they're *apes*."

"More fool them."

"The human race could be extinguished if Ryan and Tyler get out. Can *you* live with that?"

"Get in the damned car." Dax snarled, pushing him out of the door. "And never speak to me again."

"Aboot time!" Ryan beckoned to them as they left the enclosure. "We got the meter runnin here!"

His shoulders shook and he lowered his head quickly.

"Sorry. I got the hiccups in all the excitement," he laughed. "I need a good scare."

"Ah don't think that'll be a problem where we're goin," Tyler giggled.

"It's not hiccups," Frankie whispered to Dax. "He's trying to hide his cough."

"Shut up." She got behind the wheel and the boy hopped in the back.

"Remember, Frankie." Oakley turned round. "You let us do any fighting. Stay right at the back and get ready to run. Understand."

"Oh, he understands." Dax slammed the car into gear. "He understands perfectly."

She looked back, just once.

Cecelia, Ben, Susan, Otto and Dirk were clustered beside Satan, waiting sleepily for the end. They had their arms round each other, watching tendrils of smoke curling over the lip of the roof.

Dax rolled down the window and slowly held up her hand in a farewell gesture.

Then she moved off, heading towards the fire.

-44-

Yellow Leader crouched behind a low wall, sweat slicked hair sticking to his forehead.

"Yellow Leader to Brigadier Moran. We've split up and checked everywhere but the north east part of the zoo. No sign of any survivors. Over."

That was fast.

"Didn't have to bother with the centre or the south west, as both are infernos and the fire is spreading fast in all directions. The north east seems clearest but it's hard to reach when I can't breathe or see properly. I'm still trying."

Why don't you use your hazmat masks as respirators?

"They restricted our vision. Every time we put them on, one of us got struck down."

By what?

"By a fit of the giggles. What do you think?"

Watch your mouth, Yellow Leader. Predators can't be everywhere.

"They don't have to be everywhere. Only a handful of paths lead past the fire."

For Christ's sake. You have automatic weapons, rifles and grenades. You could hold off an army.

"Except we're not fighting a bloody army! The animals have picked us off, one by one. There's a tiger the size of a horse hunting me."

You don't think there are any civilians left?

"Not unless they have transport, armour, weapons and a genius leading them. Most of the creatures have headed for the north east to escape the blaze, so there's no escape that way, either."

I need your troop to check.

"Brigadier, I don't *have* any men left. I'm only heading north cause I can't get back."

What?

"You heard."

I'm sorry. You're a brave man, Yellow Leader. And a credit to your country.

"I'm not, Sir. And neither are you. Over and out."

-Part 5-

In Blair Drummond Adventure Park in Stirling, a group of chimps were seen to mourn the death of a 50-year-old female called Pansy. After she died, her daughter stayed beside her throughout the night. Later, members of the group cleaned the corpse...

Studies make a strong case that chimps not only understand the concept of death but also have ways of coping with it.

New Scientist

-45-

Sammy halted next to the Tropical Café, a little snack bar built on an observation tower, overlooking the zoo.

"What?" Bangles stared up at the circular booth. "You fancy a Snickers bar or somethin?"

"We're near the zebra paddock." Sammy slowly pulled open the door. "This place is the perfect spot to see what creatures might be waiting for us."

"What if they waiting in the café?" Bangles pointed to bloody paw prints on the stairs. "We be like a pizza delivery to them."

"Why would they stick around? Everybody up there must be dead."

"Iss your sunny disposition that keeps me hopeful, girl." Bangles pulled out his pistol. "I'll go first."

"Fire that gun and every animal in the area will hear it."

"Ok. If I meet the tiger, I'll just bitch slap it, huh?"

"You've got a knife."

"Oh yeah." The boy pulled out his switchblade. "Maybe dose critters drop dead laughin when dey see what I'm trying to defend myself with."

The pair made their way slowly up the stairs and emerged in the snack bar. It had floor to roof windows, and rows of plastic tables in the centre. A dead cook lay sprawled across one counter, head missing. There was no sign of any animals.

"You right, as always." Bangles pulled the tie from the chef's apron and fastened the handle closed. Sammy helped him push a soft drinks cabinet in front of the entrance for good measure.

Then they crept over to the window and looked out.

"Oh, snap!" the boy groaned. "Half of Africa be chillin down there."

Dozens of animals were milling around in the zebra paddock. More creatures were arriving by the second.

"They *must* know about the ladder," Sammy whimpered. "They're waiting for anyone who'll try and use it."

"Or they gots nowhere else to go, just like us. Either way, we plexed."

"Seems like it."

"Well, iss as safe here as anywheres. May as well hang an wait to be rescued."

"Or executed. Remember the choppers shooting at Brandon?"

"I don't see we gots many options."

"OK, then." Sammy sat down at a table. "Well?"

"Well, what?"

"Since we might not be alive by dinner time, you might as well buy me lunch, like you promised."

"Last supper comin up." Bangles plonked a tray of sandwiches in front of Sammy. "Pretty poor vittles but I stuck some cucumbers in em. You Brits be crazy mad about cucumber sandwiches, huh?"

"Yeah. We keep them under our bowler hats."

"Oh, thass hilarious."

"Just trying to keep your pecker up."

"I'll get you an American dictionary when this is all over. You gonna be highly embarrassed." Bangles ran to the counter and came back with a bottle of wine and two glasses. "Lookee here."

He poured them both a large measure.

"Course, I need to see some ID, fore I let you get smashed."

"Here you go." Sammy held up a middle finger. "Cheers."

They clinked glasses together.

"To good health an a long life," the boy said solemnly. "Well, more than half an hour, anyways."

"To us."

Bangles took a huge gulp.

"Hmmmmm," he smacked his lips. "This be a nasty li'l number. It gots a faint bouquet of hot dog, wid a hint of body odour."

"Let me check." Sammy leaned over the table and kissed him again. "Seems fine to me."

They grinned at each other.

"For our second date, though? I'd rather go to the movies."

"Sure. I be a big fan of creature features."

"You ever see *Lake Placid*?" Sammy took a bite of her sandwich. "That's one of my favourites. Or, it used to be…"

"Shhhhhhh."

"What?" The girl's dropped the bread onto her paper plate. "What is it?"

"The handle be movin." Bangles pulled out his knife. "Get under the table."

"Like hell." Sammy sprinted to the serving counter and grabbed a cleaver. "We're in this together."

The soft drinks cabinet squeaked across the floor as something pushed at the door. The teenagers crouched behind it ready to tackle whatever came through the gap. The apron tie stretched to breaking point.

Ready? Bangles held up his hand.

"Help me." A voice called through the crack. "I'm injured."

Sammy and Bangles stared at each other. The boy put a finger to his lips.

"Only a human would barricade themselves in here," the voice continued. "Let me in, for God's sake."

"Push your weapon through first."

"How do you know I've got one?"

"You wouldn't have made it here if you didn't."

A rifle slid into view and Sammy kicked it away.

The teenagers quickly removed the obstructions and Yellow Leader squeezed through the gap. One sleeve was lacerated and blood dripped down his arm.

"Thank you," he gasped. "My men tried to affect a rescue, but they're all dead. Except me."

The pair helped him to a chair.

"Are you the only survivors?" he asked through gritted teeth.

"Iss sure lookin that way."

"That's what I thought." The soldier pulled a pistol from inside his jacket. "Go down the stairs and into the open."

"*What*? We survive half of Noah's Ark trying to gurgitate us," Bangles got in front of Sammy. "An we gonna get sent to our maker by a meathead like you?"

"He can't fire it." Sammy peered over the boy's shoulder. "The noise will alert the animals, remember?"

"It's got a silencer," the soldier said calmly. "I really wish I didn't have to do this."

"*You* wish? I be prayin for a genie to pop outta dat wine bottle."

"You can't kill me!" Sammy scuttled away. "My dad fought in Afghanistan."

She waved a hand at Bangles.

"Shoot him. He's American."

"Breezy! Thass cold."

"Down the stairs. Both of you." The man levelled his gun at the boy. "This has to look like animals did it."

Sammy slammed both elbows on the edge of the flimsy plastic table. The other end shot up, launching their picnic into the air and hitting Yellow Leader's outstretched arm.

The bullet lodged in the ceiling as Bangles charged. He caught the bottle of wine in mid-air and swept it in an arc, smashing it over the soldier's head. The man punched the boy away and staggered backwards.

"Gnaaaaaagh!"

Sammy threw the cleaver with all her might. It buried itself in the soldier's chest. The girl clasped a hand over her mouth.

"I didn't mean it! You *made* me do that!"

Yellow Leader grasped the handle and pulled the blade out without flinching.

"Body armour, girl. Tough luck."

He swung the gun at Bangles again.

"Leave him *alone*!"

Sammy got there first and threw herself on the boy, knocking him down. Yellow Leader looked puzzled.

"Ouchie!"

"Is that a gun in your pocket?" she whispered. "Or are you just pleased I'm lying on top of you? It's hard to tell with this *thick* quilted jacket."

"Bit o both, betty."

There was a muffled whump as Bangles fired his pistol through the girl's coat.

The bullet took off the top of the soldier's ear. He yelled in pain and dived over the table, landing on the pair and scrabbling for a second Glock in his belt. Bangles and Sammy grunted as the air was forced from their bodies. The teenager tried to free his gun from the smouldering lining, but the man chopped at his wrist and the pistol clattered across the tiles.

Sammy elbowed the assailant in the nose. She arched her back, trying to throw the man off, but he was too heavy. The soldier butted her in the back of the head and her face slammed into Bangles.

"You busted my grill, Sam!"

Sammy threw her head back and crunched it into Yellow Leader's nose again, releasing a fountain of blood.

"Stop it!" He finally freed his gun and pressed it against the girl's temple. "Before I need plastic surgery."

"Oh dear," Sammy hissed. "Are our attempts to keep breathing spoiling your looks?"

"Just stay *still*."

They lay in a pile, breathing heavily.

"Well, *this* be different," Bangles mumbled through a split lip.

"How old are you both?" Yellow Leader rasped.

"Fifteen," Sammy grunted. "And trying our best to reach sixteen."

"Ah, shit." The man rolled off and holstered his weapon.

"I can't do this."

-46-

Yellow Leader got to his feet and helped the teenagers up.

"I'm not going to harm you." He raised his arms in surrender. "I didn't enlist to carry out this kind of job."

"No frontin?" Bangles dusted himself down. "You aint gonna cap us?"

"I don't think you guys *can* be killed. I try again and I'll probably get hit by a bolt of lightning."

"Boom ting! Thass the lick!"

"What did he just say?" Yellow Leader squinted at Sammy.

"He's pleased with the turn of events." The girl returned his stare. "Why would you have orders to kill us? We haven't done anything wrong."

"It's not about you."

"So *why*?"

"A meteor called THX4 came down in the zoo last night," Yellow Leader said. "We've been secretly tracking it but we got the wrong place."

"*That's* what mutated the animals."

"Yeah. And if it could make *them* stronger and smarter, think what it could do to troops? It's *the*

291

perfect weapon. My bosses think it's worth killing a few survivors in here to keep that secret."

"Depends on where you standing," Bangles grumbled

"To be fair, we didn't expect anyone to *be* standing," the soldier replied. "The army genuinely thought nobody was left alive. But I was leading a mop up crew, just in case."

"Charming."

"Not that me disobeying orders will do you much good." The man fetched his rifle. "It's Armageddon outside."

"There's a knotted rope ladder a few hundred yards from here." Sammy led him to the window. "If we could get to it, we'd be out."

"Only there be a few obstacles in the way," Bangles added. "I can see lions hidden in the grass. We go near that rope an they be all up in our Kool-Aid."

"There's also part of my black ops team patrolling on the other side of the wall." The soldier removed his helmet and rubbed his hair. "With instructions to shoot on sight."

"Say *what* now?"

Yellow Leader winked. "I can take care of them, at least."

He pulled a walkie talkie from his belt.

"Yellow Leader to Red Leader," he said. "I'm in the tower café at the north east wall. I'm too injured to move fast, but I spotted a couple of people heading for the south side of the zoo, skirting the fire and carrying a plank. I presume they intend to place it against the wall and escape. Move the perimeter patrol down there ASAP to intercept them.

Will do, sir.

"Excellent. Over and out." The soldier turned off his radio

"There goes my chances of promotion."

He gave Bangles and Sammy a half-hearted smile.

"Red team are now heading south to stop a non-existent escape. Even if they hear us trying to fight our way out, they'll assume it's me making a last stand. It will give you a few minutes grace to get into the woods before they realise their mistake."

"You busted some phatty moves there, braw!" Bangles tapped his heart. "Respect."

"Yeah. Didn't get that either, but here's the plan." The soldier picked up his rifle and opened a window. "Go outside and hide in the bushes."

"And you?"

"I'll start shooting and draw as many animals towards me as I can. There's only one way into this café, up the stairs. I can hold an army off until I run out of ammo."

"The animals aint all gonna attack you and leave the rope unguarded." Bangles unfastened the sash. "They *smart.*"

"You won't need the ladder." Yellow Leader pulled a grenade from his belt and handed it to Sammy, along with his pistol. "Just reach the nearest part of the wall. Pull the pin and you'll have ten seconds to hit the deck. This baby will blow a hole big enough for you to get through. I'll try to stop the animals catching up. If they come through the gap after you, though, you're on your own."

"The animals won't pass the perimeter," Sammy assured him. "They've reclaimed what they see as their territory. Now they'll stay and defend it."

"If you say so." The man rubbed his stubbled chin. "But here's a word of advice. There's no way a handgun will bring down a big cat, especially a mutated one. They get that close, you'd be better using them on each other."

"We owe you one, bro," Bangles shook his hand "What's your name, anyway?"

"Yellow Leader is fine."

"Thass a bit unfortunate."

"Yeah. My obituary writers will have a field day."

"Didn't you say you were alone?" Sammy's face clouded.

"Yes. My squad are all dead, luckily for you."

"You sure?" Bangles cocked his head. "Cause I can hear a vehicle."

"It's the rest of them." The girl gasped. "They're alive too!"

"What the hell are you guys made of?" Yellow Leader shook his head. "Kevlar?"

"You know it, braw!"

"All the same, stick to the plan." He waved the pair away. "I'll do what I can to help."

"They don't stand a chance, do they?"

"No. But you might. Get *going*."

"C'mon Sammy." Bangles grabbed her arm. "We ghostin. Aim true, soldier blue. Peace out."

He kissed the girl's cheek and pulled her through the door.

"Young love, eh?" Yellow Leader braced his rifle on the window sill.

"I suppose that's something worth fighting for."

-47-

Dax headed north, hunched over the steering wheel. Her passengers were thrown from side to side, bracing themselves against the doors and windows. Before them, a barrier of flame obscured the road.

"You're not..." Oakley covered his face with both arms. "You wouldn't!"

"I am." Dax kept going. "And I *will*."

The car roared into the firestorm. On either side, a searing orange heat blistered the paint and licked at the windows.

Then it burst into the sunlight, trailing a plume of smoke.

"You trying tae barbecue us, you wee hellcat?" Ryan pounded on the rear window. "I feel like a can o baked beans!"

The girl ignored him, roaring along the empty paths, leaving the conflagration behind.

"Zebra paddock is up ahead." She headed for the gate. "Hold on."

The police car burst through the wooden barrier, splintering it into pieces. It careened over the grass, wheels throwing up gobs of dirt.

"This is bad." The girl slewed to a halt. "This is *very* bad."

Between the teenagers and the ladder were hundreds of animals.

"We have to go back!" Oakley pleaded. "I'm not into committing suicide."

"Back to the fire, yeah?"

"We could circle around the perimeter and try the entrance again."

"We're here and these animals are flesh and blood." Dax gunned the engine. "This is a metal box."

She flipped a switch.

"With flashing lights."

"You're insane, aren't you?"

"Getting there." She floored the accelerator.

The car lurched forwards as a herd of zebras raced to meet them. It ploughed into the mass, flinging them aside. The bumper buckled and steam began to pour from the radiator. Dax headed for the wall, lips set in a grim line.

"Hippo!"

The gigantic beast lumbered towards the car, prepared to meet it head on. Dax swerved at the last second and roared past. The hippo sideswiped the vehicle, almost lifting it from the ground. One hubcap flew off and rolled across the grass. Ryan and Tyler clutched at each other, trying not to be jolted out of the boot. The creature gave a bellow and collapsed, leg broken by the impact.

A jaguar leapt onto the bonnet and was swept away by the momentum.

"This is too easy!" Dax thumped the steering wheel. "Is *that* all you got?"

"Try not to tempt fate, D." Oakley had turned green.

The side passenger window exploded as a vulture crashed through it. Siobhan fired her pistol into the wrinkled head and it dropped away.

A pack of wolves were racing alongside the vehicle, tongues lolling, unsure of how to stop the juggernaut.

"We are *so* getting there!" the girl shouted. "I can see the ladder!"

Suddenly the car soared over the edge of a small crevasse. It churned through a stream and collided with the bank on the other side. The occupants were thrown forwards, as the vehicle came to a grinding halt, mangled bonnet buried in soil.

"A ditch!" Oakley unfastened his seat belt. "We plough our way through half of God's bloody creation and we get stopped by a *ditch*?"

"Out now!" Siobhan kicked open her door. "We're still armed."

They scrambled up the incline as the rest of the animals closed in. Ryan and Tyler followed, weighed down by their armour, pulling off gauntlets in order to operate the guns properly.

"Form a circle," Ryan commanded. "Don't fire until you cannae miss."

"Miss? I could shut my eyes and hit something!" Oakley paused. "Actually, that's not a bad idea."

"Get intae the middle, wee man." Tyler pushed Frankie behind him. "I'll no let you die."

There was a crack from far away and one of the wolves fell. Then another. And another.

"We've got help!" Siobhan swept damp hair from her eyes, suddenly rejuvenated. "Someone's shooting from up in that café."

The remaining wolves rushed the group.

Oakley swept his automatic rifle in an arc, teeth chattering with the recoil. The predators ran into a hail of bullets, cutting them to pieces.

"Keep moving towards the ladder. Whoever is up there is a crack shot and he's hitting all the most dangerous animals."

One by one, the larger creatures were being cut down by Yellow Leader.

Seeing that their enemy stood a chance of escaping, every beast charged at once.

"This is it." Dax narrowed her eyes. "We stand or fall, right here."

The teenagers knelt and let loose with everything they had. Spent cartridges flew into the air and the group was enveloped by oily vapour. The heat from their guns turned the air into a shimmering curtain as they loaded and fired. Loaded and fired.

They kept their fingers on the triggers until the chambers of their weapons finally spun empty.

When the smoke cleared, they stood up. The paddock was littered with carcasses, large and small. The remaining creatures slunk away north east, finally defeated.

"There's the ladder." Ryan coughed loudly and wiped gunpowder residue from his eyes. "Nothin left tae stop us now, lads."

"Are you all right?" Dax asked sharply.

"Course not. I havnae had a ciggie for aboot three hours."

"Look." Tyler pushed up his visor. "A mannie in that tower is waving tae us."

"Dinnae be rude, then." Ryan raised his arm in a friendly greeting. "Wave back."

-48-

In the café, Yellow Leader opened the window as far as it would go.

"Stay away from the wall!" he bellowed. "There are lions hiding in the long grass!"

He was too far away to be heard and it was pointless trying to shoot the big cats. They were just out of range.

Yellow Leader reloaded, then climbed up on the window sill and indicated with his rifle. The teenagers signalled happily back.

"Stay there!" he shouted again, though he knew he couldn't be heard. "I'm coming!"

As he turned to clamber back inside, the door of the snack bar burst open, knocked off its hinges by the sheer bulk of the intruder.

"Ah. You finally caught up with me again."

Sheridan bounded over the tables, claws clicking on the Formica surfaces. Yellow Leader tried to bring up his rifle, but it hit the window latch, knocking him off balance. He dropped the weapon and it spiralled towards the ground.

The soldier teetered on the sill, arms windmilling.

"Shit."

He closed his eyes and toppled backwards.

"That numpty's fallen oot." Tyler's jaw dropped. "What a dunderhead."

"Nothin we can do about it, eh?." Ryan wheezed. "C'mon lads. Let's get goin."

"I think he was trying to warn us about something," Frankie said. "But what?"

"The café prices?" Ryan clunked towards the rope. "Who cares?"

"Wait." The child held him back. "That was too easy."

"It didnae seem easy!"

"Oakley?" Frankie asked urgently. "What are the biggest draws in any zoo?"

"I don't know. Lions?"

"Do you spot any dead lions in this mess?"

"Eh… no."

"Then they're still alive."

"I cannae see them, wee man," Ryan pointed out.

"Neither can I. That's the problem." Frankie looked apprehensively around. "But there's a lot of long grass around that ladder. The kind of terrain big cats use to hide."

His little face fell.

"They're not going to make the same mistake as the other animals," he said bitterly.

"They're *waiting* for us."

From nearby bushes, Sammy and Bangles watched Yellow Leader plummet to his death. The girl covered her eyes before he hit the ground.

"Let's move out, girl." Bangles tugged at the girl's ruined coat. "Dude bought it for sure."

"He was trying to warn the others about the lions," Sammy said. "We've got to do it instead."

"For real?" The boy stroked her hair. "We juss about used up all our chances."

"Help the rest. That's what you said."

"Yeah. I got a big mouth, don't I?"

"Get his rifle," Sammy begged. "I can't look at him."

"Aw'ight. Stay hidden." Bangles ran over the body.

Yellow Leader lay broken on the ground, helmet cracked in two. The boy scooped up his weapon, then knelt and checked for a pulse. There was none.

"Rest easy, Yellow." He let go of the man's wrist. "You was beasty when we needed you."

He spotted a last grenade, fastened to the man's belt, and gently removed it.

"You the gift that keeps on givin, dude. God bless."

He looked up in time to see Sheridan rounding the corner of the tower.

"Oh, snap. I am *jacked*."

Bangles glanced at Sammy, still hidden in the bushes. She hadn't seen the predator.

Get over here, the girl signalled. *What are you waiting for?*

Bangles couldn't lead the tiger towards her and doubted he could hit anything with a rifle he'd never held before. He spotted the acacia tree. It was the closest thing to safety within sprinting distance.

"Hey Tigger!" he yelled. "Over here! You and me be dancin O.G. style."

Then he raced for the tree.

"Bangles!" Sammy screamed. "What are you doing? Come back!"

Sheridan headed after the boy, gathering speed with every bound. Bangles pulled the pin on the grenade and dropped it as he ran.

"Cheez," he rasped, stumbling over the uneven ground. "I eaten too many corn dogs to be executin *dese* moves."

The grenade went off, just as Sheridan was passing it. The explosion flipped the big cat into the air and it came down on its back with a sickening whump, sending up a cloud of dust.

"Didn't land on you feet *this* time." Bangles picked up a stone and launched it at the beast. It bounced off the banded hide, but Sheridan didn't move.

"Say my name, stripy!" The boy did a little dance. "I am your *daddy*!"

He reached the acacia and climbed into the branches.

"Well… I be back in the tree."

He bent down and picked up the video camera he had discarded that morning.

"Jeezie peeps." He held up the VCR with a grin. "This be my lucky day. I'll get a *billion* hits on YouTube now."

Sammy finally let out her breath.

"You made it," she laughed. "You crazy fool."

She tucked the remaining grenade gingerly into her jacket and began to edge through the undergrowth towards the others.

"My turn now."

-49-

The others watched Bangle's narrow escape in disbelief.

"I'd given up on him," Dax grinned. "No sign of Sammy though."

"It doesn't help our predicament," Oakley reminded her. "What do we do about whatever's waiting for us?"

"They don't know we're out of bullets, or they'd already be heading this way." Frankie's eyes darted from side to side. "If we move, they might see it as a retreat and attack anyway."

"So, it's a stalemate."

"We can't just stand here like a bunch of carnival ducks," Dax snapped.

"I'm thinking!"

"Bangles has the video camera." Siobhan was staring hungrily at the boy. "I've got to get my hands on it."

"You gone soft in the head?" Ryan stuck the sword in the ground and pushed up his visor. "We have tae stick together."

"It's the proof I need."

"He's got a rifle too." Dax dropped her own empty weapon and beckoned to him. "Bangles! Over here!"

The boy shouted back but the wind whipped his words away. Instead, he gestured wildly in the opposite direction.

"What's he doing?" Dax stamped her foot. "Why won't he leave the tree?"

"I'm guessing he can see everything from up there," Frankie replied. "I was right. There are predators hidden by the ladder."

Bangles was pointing to the tower, urging them to flee in that direction.

"I've got to get that camera before he takes off again." Siobhan broke into a run. "I'll be right back."

"I'll go with her and fetch the rifle." Dax sprinted after her companion.

"Dax, no!" Frankie clutched at her and missed. "The enemy will think we're running away!"

But the girls were already racing towards the acacia.

"Pussy alert, lads," Tyler whispered. "To your right."

A dozen tawny backs were moving slowly towards them through the grass.

"Keep your weapon up, Oakley," Frankie said. "The swords will make them cautious, but that automatic rifle is the thing they're really wary of."

"It's empty!"

"They don't know that or they'd be charging us right now."

"The girls are almost at the tree," the boy raised the gun to his shoulder. "Hurry up, Dax. We need some firepower."

"Wassup, ladies?" Bangles helped the girls into the acacia. "Never thought I'd set peepers on you again."

"Can I have the camera?" Siobhan panted. "I need to film this."

"Guh. It cost me £50."

"I'll owe you."

"Make it £60 and it's yours."

"Done."

"And the rifle," Dax added. "We're out of ammo."

"I reckon you know how to use it better than me." The boy handed it over and pulled out his pistol. "I'll stick wid my gat."

He gave a weary sigh.

"You gonna ax for my threads while you at it? Cause I aint gonna lock up wid dose critters in juss my C.K. briefs."

"Come with us. We're going to try for the ladder."

"Cheah. About that?" Bangles jerked a thumb at the wall. "The army gots orders to shoot anyone escaping…"

"*What*?"

"*And* there be lions hidden near the ladder."

"We just figured that out. But the rest of the animals retreated back into the zoo. There's no other way to escape."

"You think?" The boy gave a triumphant grin. "I'm guessing my honey be about to change all dat."

"Hey guys!" Sammy shouted from the bushes. "Making you a new exit!"

She pulled the pin on her grenade and hurled it at the wall. The device exploded, blasting the brickwork to smithereens.

"You little beauty!" Ryan punched the air. "Bottle of Buckfast for that girl!"

Oakley headed for the gap, dragging Frankie behind. Ryan and Tyler lumbered after them like metal marionettes.

The pride burst from their hiding place and gave chase.

Dax sighted the rifle and fired. The recoil almost knocked her out of the tree, but she wedged herself between two branches and aimed again. One lion went down. Then another. They slowed to a halt and sank into the undergrowth again, moving cautiously forward on their bellies.

Sammy looked towards Bangles.

"Go through the gap, kiddo." The boy clasped his hands together. "I'll be fine. I'll catch you up. Just go *through*."

The girl faltered. Then she began to crawl towards the tree, using the grass as cover.

-50-

Oakley reached the jagged 'V' where Sammy's grenade had blasted away the upper part of the wall and scrambled up the rubble, dragging Frankie along. He hoisted the child over the top and Frankie jumped down to the track on the other side. Oakley reached back to help Ryan and Tyler.

"Free and clear!" Ryan scrambled up the incline towards him, panting loudly.

A burly hand landed on the boy's shoulder.

"It's no often folk like us get tae be superheroes, Wee Pounder." Tyler pulled his friend back. "We're no leavin anybody behind."

"I dinnae want tae be a superhero." Ryan tried to scramble through the hole again. "I want tae *live*."

"Aw right, then. Bugger off." Tyler turned his back on the boy. "Ahm staying tae help the others."

"For God's sake, Ty. We've never been the good guys. Why should we change now? We can escape!"

"Tae whit? A life o thieving or stacking supermarket shelves?" Tyler shook his head. "An we winnae even get the chance tae do that, will we?"

He tapped his friend's chest.

"Yiv got the disease, Ryan. The one the kiddie was talkin aboot."

"I dinnae!"

"Aye, you do. You're wheezing like yiv smoked a joint the size o a carrot."

Ryan looked up longingly at Oakley's outstretched hand.

"Besides, those girls are depending on us." Tyler pressed home his advantage. "And they *are* seriously hot."

Ryan glanced across at the tree.

"Are they *filmin* this?"

"You better believe it. We'll get mair internet hits than *Gangnam Style*."

"Well, why did you no *say* so?" Ryan winked at Oakley. "Look after that wee pest."

He climbed back down.

"Better make sure they get my best side, bud. Wait. That's any side, cause I'm a handsome bugger, eh?"

"You've got a helmet on, Ry." Tyler pressed his armoured head against his friend's. "Still, I knew you wouldnae leave me behind, though. We're mates."

"Aye. Dinnae get soppy, yah dick."

The boys turned to face their attackers.

"Time tae lose yir temper, big man," Ryan punched his friend's arm. "We'll kick so much yellow arse, folk winnae be able tae see the sky fur bums."

"You said it, pal."

Oakley watched from the top of the rubble as they marched towards the lions.

Nearing the tree, Sammy raised her head to get proper bearings.

"Keep down, Sam!" Bangles pleaded. "They'll *see* you."

It was too late. One of the lions broke away from the pride and streaked after her.

"No! No, no, no!" Bangles leapt out of the tree and sprinted towards the girl. "Move it, betty! You been clocked."

Sammy jumped to her feet and began to run. Then her eyes widened.

"Bangles! The tiger!"

Sheridan had risen groggily to its feet. It exhaled slowly and shook its filthy mane. Then it loped after the boy.

"Big cats gaining on Bangles and Sammy!" Siobhan thumped Dax on the shoulder. "Drop them."

Dax aimed and fired, too fast

The lion grunted in pain and stumbled. But it recovered and kept going.

"Again!"

"That was my last bullet!"

Bangles and Sammy pulled out their handguns as they drew closer. But the predators jinked and weaved behind them, using the teens as shields. And, as Yellow

Leader had pointed out, pistols were no defence against big cats.

The pair skidded to a halt, a few feet from each other.

"Don't let me die this way, Bangles," Sammy pleaded. "Please."

The boy stopped and raised his gun, trying to aim around her at the lion. It was no use. Sheridan gave a satisfied growl as he bore down on Bangles.

"Look into my eyes, Sam," the boy said softly. "Don't be scared, huh?"

"Bye, boo." Sammy touched her lips with one finger and blew him a kiss. "Maybe I should have stayed invisible after all."

"On my count. One. Two… Three."

As the creatures prepared to leap, they both fired.

-51-

Dax and Siobhan watched helplessly as the big cats skirted the bodies of Sammy and Bangles and turned their attention to the tree. They began to inch towards the girls, still wary of the rifle, unaware it was empty.

Siobhan began filming their approach.

"You never give in, do you?" Dax began scrambling up through the branches. "We've got to get higher."

Oakley watched them climb, face white and fists clenched.

"Come on, Will!" Frankie's voice drifted up from the other side of the wall. "You're almost out!"

"I can't."

"There's nothing you can do to help Dax and Siobhan!" The child was hopping up and down. "You don't have a weapon."

"I hate Jelly Babies, Frankie," Oakley sighed. "Always have."

"*What*?"

"I threw away the sweet you gave me when you weren't looking." The boy rolled up his sleeve, revealing red blotches on his arm. He leaned over and peered down at the child. "Good luck, kid."

"No! *Oakley*! Come back!"

Oakley picked up two chunks of rubble studded with broken glass. Then he scrambled down and ran towards the tree.

The injured lion turned to face the new foe, leaving Sheridan to tackle the girls. As the tiger began to climb up the trunk, powerful claws digging into the bark, the lion charged.

Oakley waited, arms outstretched, until it reached him. Then he slammed both rocks together on its head. He went down, still pounding at the beast, fighting until the last breath had left his body. The lion slunk away, blood pouring from its lacerated muzzle. After a few yards, it collapsed.

The rest of the pride had surrounded Ryan and Tyler. The teenagers hacked and chopped, armour protecting them from the aggressors' fangs. But sheer numbers finally overwhelmed them.

Ryan succumbed first, his neck broken by a brutal swipe. Tyler continued to fight alone, straddling his prone friend.

"Kill my best bud, ya tossers?" He was a one-man army, bellowing with rage as he kicked and slashed. "I'll cut you! I'll screw you up! C'mon! C'MON!"

The last of the pride swept Tyler off his feet, fastened mighty jaws on his helmet and bit. With his last breath, the teenager thrust his sword into the beast's chest. They died, locked together.

"I can't get any higher!" Dax and Siobhan had wormed their way through the thickest tangle of branches and were now wedged on a fork, fifteen feet up.

"Neither can the tiger, thank Christ."

Sheridan was still trying to reach them but the foliage was too dense for its bulk. It slid down a few feet, lacerating the bark with its claws. Finally, it dropped to the ground. It sniffed the air and gave a throaty bark. Then it headed across the paddock and leapt through the gap in the wall.

"Sammy said the animals weren't interested in escaping!" Siobhan rasped.

"This one's different." Dax slammed a hand into the wood. "It's *the* alpha predator and it can't reach us, so it's going after Frankie."

"We've got to stop it."

"Got one more beast to contend with first."

The last lion pulled itself upright and slunk towards the acacia, letting out a bone shaking roar. Its back legs gave way and the beast crumpled again, tongue protruding over bloody black lips.

"It's badly injured, thanks to Oakley." Dax began to lower herself down. "You head for the ladder and I'll go for the gap in the wall. It can't catch us both."

"*That's* your plan?"

"I could just push you out and run while he's tearing you apart."

"Know what? I believe you." Siobhan tucked the camera into her waistband. "What's your real name, anyway? My readers will want to know."

"It's Ethel." The girl gave an awkward smile. "Never really forgave my parents for that."

"No kidding. I'll stick with Dax."

Siobhan jumped from the acacia and headed for the rope. Dax followed, running for the demolished wall.

The lion looked from one girl to the other. Then it struggled upright and limped after Siobhan. But its movements were slow and laboured.

Dax reached the wall and turned.

"Faster!" she urged. "He's too badly hurt to catch up."

Siobhan hit the ladder in mid stride and began to climb.

"Oh, yes!" Dax grinned. "Humans one. Animals nil."

But the rope ladder was unstable, swaying from side to side. Siobhan's foot slipped and she swung round, crashing into the wall, desperately clinging on. The VCR was jolted from her waistband and tumbled to the ground.

The girl regained her footing but Dax saw her shoulders stiffen.

"No!" She cried. "Don't go back for that. *Don't*!"

Siobhan looked up. Safety was only feet away. She hung on the ladder for a few seconds. Then she let go and dropped back down.

The lion summoned the last of its fading strength and put on a spurt. Siobhan scrabbled around in the grass trying to find the camera.

"Got it!"

She scooped up the device and attempted to climb, using only one hand.

The dying cat soared through the air, talons outstretched. It slammed into the girl, knocking her from the wall. Siobhan tried to throw the precious VCR over the top, but jagged teeth fastened on her torso. The camera bounced off the brickwork and landed on its side, filming the death throes of the lion and a girl who had come so close to the story of the century.

"GOD DAMMIT!" Dax yelled. "Why did you have to be so frigging... *noble*?"

The camera was only a hundred yards away and there was nothing left alive between her and the device. Dead animals and humans were strewn across the grass in a fleshy red mosaic.

Taking a deep breath, she ran towards her companion, hopping unceremoniously over the corpses. When she reached Siobhan, Dax ran a hand through her dirty, gore slicked hair.

"Forgive me," she whispered.

She brought her boot down on the VCR, over and over, until it splintered into pieces. Siobhan watched through sightless eyes.

"You're right of, course. The truth deserves to come out." Dax knelt and stroked the girl's face. "But I can't let that happen."

She ran back, climbed through the gap and went looking for Frankie.

-52-

Dax pushed her way through the undergrowth, trying to make as little noise as possible. Reaching a small clearing, she spotted Frankie, splayed against the trunk of an oak tree, trying to blend into the scenery. He sucked in air when he saw the girl.

"Run!" he hissed. " Sheridan is hunting me."

"I'm sorely tempted to let him continue." Dax advanced on the child. "But too many good people lost their lives to get you this far."

Frankie licked his lips, eyes like saucers. "Dax. He's behind you."

The girl slowly turned, hairs rising on her neck. Sheridan was crouched on the other side of the clearing, licking his lips in anticipation.

The girl reached the tree in two strides.

"Get behind me." She pushed Frankie out of the way, grabbed a stout stick off the ground and took up a defensive stance.

It was a useless gesture. The big cat could splinter the puny weapon with one snap of its jaws.

"No." The child slid out of her shadow and raised his small fists. "I'll fight by your side."

"You're serious, yeah?"

"I've got a white belt in karate."

Sheridan advanced on them, a trail of saliva dripping from its yellow fangs.

"I mean it, kid. Run. Before *I* do."

"Make me."

The tiger charged, mouth open in a silent snarl. As it reached the girl, a huge bough fell from the oak and landed on the creature, knocking it flat.

Straddling it was Brandon Golledge, meteor fragment in his fist. Sheridan tried to crawl from under the foliage, spraying spittle in all directions. The boy slammed the rock down on the tiger's skull as hard as he could.

The beast roared in agony. Dax thrust her home made spear into the open maw. Brandon struck again and again. Even Frankie joined in, punching and kicking the animal.

Eyes misting over, Sheridan finally collapsed, splayed out like a huge Victorian rug.

"Thanks for the help, girl." Brandon stood up and dusted himself off. "That was a pretty hairy moment."

"Brandon! I can't believe it!" Dax ran forwards and threw her arms around him. Then she recoiled.

Brandon felt strange. His torso was solid as wood and his eyes were no longer brown but golden, so bright they almost glowed.

"But... you were dead." The girl backed away. "I saw you get fried, yeah?"

"He was carrying the meteor fragment when he used the Tasers," Frankie explained. "Their voltage must have generated a *huge* amount of heat. Enough for the meteor to mutate him before the water cooled it again."

He sounded awe struck.

"Brandon's virtually indestructible now. Exactly the kind of person the military wanted to create."

"I do feel pretty good." The boy flexed his muscles. "But I doubt I'll be joining the armed forces."

"How did you get out of the zoo?"

"Jumped on the wall and tore the barbed wire apart." He held out lacerated hands, already beginning to heal. "I appear to be tougher and more... agile than I once was."

He grinned

"I bumped into Frankie first and we could hear some big creature crashing about, so the kid set a trap, with him as bait."

"I learned that trick from the animals." Frankie gave Sheridan a kick.

Brandon looked around.

"So... Where *is* everyone?"

"We're all that's left."

Frankie turned his head away.

"Really?" For the first time, the boy's demeanour slipped. "*Nobody* else made it?"

"All dead." Dax pointed at the fragment in Brandon's hand. "Because of that lump of rock."

"It was in the rucksack everyone was yelling about," the boy said. "Figured it must be important, so I brought it with me."

"Siobhan is dead too?" Frankie's face crumpled.

"I'm afraid so."

"You're right, Dax." The boy sank to his knees and wept. "*Everything* is my fault."

"Hey. That's how *I* usually feel." The girl put her arm gingerly around him. "Look. We did what we had to do. Now we live with it."

She held him until his sobbing subsided.

"I don't know what you're both talking about." Brandon scratched his head. "But we should make ourselves scarce. You can explain on the way."

"With pleasure." Dax let Frankie go. "But there's something we have to do first."

They stood at the edge of the nearby quarry. A wide expanse of silted green water stretched away in front of them. Brandon still held the bloody fragment in his hand.

"Can I do the honours?" Frankie asked. "I'd like to finish what I started."

"I can throw pretty far, but knock yourself out."

Frankie launched the rock into the air. It soared for a hundred yards before vanishing under the surface. Dax gasped and Brandon whistled appreciatively.

"I'm a lot stronger too," Frankie said miserably. "The army can search the zoo from here till eternity. They'll never find what they're looking for."

"What now?" Dax asked Brandon.

"Apparently, my face is all over the TV." The teenager shrugged. "I better lie low for a while. Nobody is going to miss me."

"Same here," Frankie added quietly. "I've no family left."

"Then, I suppose you're stuck with me." Brandon nudged him. "Looks like I have a sidekick."

"All superheroes need one, don't they?" Frankie turned to Dax "What about you?"

"I'll sneak home and get cleaned up." The girl wiped at her bloodstained clothing. "Say I skipped the ceremony and didn't go to the zoo – which would be just like me. I got a perfect alibi, after all."

"What's that?" Brandon asked.

"I don't have any bloody plague, yeah?"

"But Siobhan filmed us in the zoo," Frankie reminded her. "What if the army find her camera?"

"You don't need to worry about that," she said softly.

"Oh." Frankie understood immediately.

"I hope my parents aren't home." Dax suddenly looked lost. "They may not lie to cover for me. We don't exactly get along."

"Think so?" Brandon gave a bark of laughter. "Your mum and dad were trying to get over the wall and save you, despite believing they'd be infected."

"They were?" The girl's eyes widened. "*Really*?"

"It's the reason I came back." Brandon smiled wanly at the girl. "Couldn't stand to watch their pain and do nothing about it."

"You're kidding?" A huge grin spread across Dax's face.

"They're in police custody. Waiting and hoping. Go home and get changed. Say you were never in the place. They'll be over the moon."

Dax swallowed hard. "Who the hell *are* you?"

"It's a long story and I don't have time to tell it."

"I have to go find my mum and dad." The girl wiped tears from her eyes. "Will you both be all right?"

"I think so." Frankie looked timidly up at her. "Thank you for saving me."

"Give me a hug, mastermind." The girl held out her arms. "And take care of this guy. Not that he needs it."

"Yeah," Brandon grunted. "So everybody says."

Frankie ran over and squeezed Dax tightly.

"I only tried to do what…"

"Shhhh." The girl embraced him. "Let's not go there. Ever."

"Only in my nightmares." Frankie let go. "Bye Dax."

"You know, I finally figured out what separates human beings from the other animals." Dax touched his cheek gently, careful not to leave a bloody smear. "Absolutely nothing."

She headed into the trees without looking back.

"So?" Brandon turned to the child. "You're seven. But you have a brain the size of a planet. That about right?"

"Yup."

"Think you could figure out how to rob a casino?" He ruffled Frankie's hair. "Don't worry, I'm only kidding."

"Actually, I probably could." The boy thought for a second. "We'll need money, won't we? If we're on the run."

Brandon looked at his hands. They were sure and steady, as they always were before he did something insane.

"Frankie?"

"Yes?"

"I think this is the beginning of a beautiful friendship."

END

The video [recorded by a visitor] shows the chimp pointing its finger at a window bolt and mimicking the movement required to open it. In one gesture, its interlaced fingers are reminiscent of the sign language for the word 'gate'. A visitor can be heard saying 'He wants us to lift the window up.'

The Telegraph

All 112 baboons at Holland's Emmen Zoo have turned their backs on visitors this week, refusing to eat and baffling zoologists.

The Guardian Newspaper

Katie Slocombe of the University of York and her team recorded vocalisations by a group of adult chimps from the Netherlands before and after their relocation to Edinburgh Zoo. Three years after the move, Dutch chimps had picked up the pronunciations of their Scottish hosts.

New Scientist Magazine

One Bonobo ape sharpened a stick with her teeth to fashion a spear and jabbed it at the researcher.

New Scientist Magazine

ABOUT THE AUTHOR

Jan-Andrew Henderson (J.A. Henderson) is the author of 40 teenage, YA, adult and non-fiction books. Published in the UK, USA, Canada, Australia and Europe, he has been shortlisted for fifteen literary awards and is the winner of the Doncaster Book Prize, The Aurealis Award and the Royal Mail Award.

www.janandrewhenderson.com